SPORTING WITH AMARYLLIS

SPORTING WITH AMARYLLIS

PAUL WEST

THE OVERLOOK PRESS

WOODSTOCK • NEW YORK

First published in the United States in 1996 by
The Overlook Press
Lewis Hollow Road
Woodstock, New York 12498

Library of Congress Cataloging-in-Publications Data

West, Paul, 1930-
Sporting with Amaryllis / Paul West.
p. cm.
1. Milton, John, 1608-1674--Relations with women--Fiction.
2. Poets, English--Early modern, 1500-1700--Fiction. I. Title
PR6073.E766S66   1966   813'.54--dc20   96-22766
ISBN 0-87951-666-6

BOOK DESIGN AND FORMATTING BY BERNARD SCHLEIFER

Printed in the United States of America

First Edition

10 9 8 7 6 5 4 3 2 1

I'm missing neither reedy old Cambridge nor the lodgings that used to be mine. . . . My, time and again I've seen girls with bodies that made my head swim and would give a hard-on to God Almighty. Ah, those eyes, like the flashing stars that poles roll around in, and those ivory necks! Really, London women have it all.

JOHN MILTON, *Elegy I,* to Charles Diodati,
April 1626, 10-11, 51-56, 71

Were it not better done as others use,
To sport with Amaryllis in the shade,
Or with the tangles of Neaera's hair?

Lycidas, November 1637, 67-69

SPORTING WITH AMARYLLIS

EVEN AT THEIR WETTEST, HIS EYES COULD BE SURLY, AND when the heavy upper lids slid down he had sealed you away, unworthy of further insult. He was only seventeen, but Chappell his tutor scolded him for not being sleek enough, for not adapting himself to the whims of his elders. Smart, gifted, busy, retentive, but somewhat brash, he let his emotions get the better of him, complaining (as if there could be any changing of it) about the dryrot curriculum that represented the human creature at its deadest and most barren. He boasted too, in a reverse way, claiming that from the age of twelve he had virtually blinded himself, poring over books until midnight as if pursuing a life sentence prematurely. He never smiled much and prided himself on being truculent without being belligerent; he knew his Latin only too well and could distinguish between being fierce and being warlike in a trice. In those old Roman words, he claimed, he could hear the throats of long-gone ancestors, all the way back to proto-language, in which the bawl, the bleat, the whine became consistent vocal shapes. His father had schooled him in music; his school, St. Paul's, had equipped him with Latin, Greek, and Hebrew; and private tutors had seeded him with French and Italian. Where else should such a little monster go but Cambridge? Later centuries would have dubbed him a swot, which is to say *studies with obvious tedium*. He heard the music of humanity all right, but not in the programs of Scholastic logic designed to ready him for becoming a clergyman.

No, in his mind's eye he was too much a pagan, treading water at Cambridge while wondering how to escape the preambles to reverence. He was a sensitive, fine soul alert to the pleasures of being green, a tyro, an amateur, unwilling to close his mind before it had been tempted, and remarking in himself, with mild derision, what he sometimes referred to as the faint subterfuges of untutored eloquence. Half the time, when he spoke, the words volunteered themselves, coming from he knew not where but having little to do with the body that heaved and perspired, the nose that bled, the hands that flexed their fingers, the eyes that ached and ran. A ball of air within his chest gave him pangs and only sometimes melted away, punctured, he thought, by crumbs.

If only, like his father the moneylender, he could become a composer, but to music he was a receiver, a staunch devourer, too much in love with it to make it behave on the page or in the air. He was too ready to unfurl his arm and make his fingers taper as a singularly poignant phrase affected him, most often from an organ; music made him strike attitudes of almost ineffable buoyancy, and he was aware of them too, smirking even as he overdid the histrionics of appreciation. He sang too, with wavering solemnity, and a bad habit of sticking his index finger in an ear to make his voice more resonant to himself. Music, he said, ran up the stem of life and popped out as a flower. Music was breath on fire, eternity made momentary. It put him in mind of the ancient Greek who, chopped into mincemeat for the gods, was at last put back together, except for a piece of shoulder already eaten (a goddess in a hurry). Ivory replaced the missing flesh. Ivory was music, of what music had done to anatomy. So, he mused, he was a little horror for thinking such things, for linking the majesty of music to the expendability of meat. He was not normal, he knew, but he was not a genius yet, as Chappell said, instructing him to read all of a certain text and come prepared to construe any portion of it, even while the whole of literature waited in the scullery like a vagrant promised a meal of bread and stale beef.

"You shall be said, John," Chappell told him. "There is only the work, then the ministry. Do not look too far for fear of toppling in."

"No," the young polymath answered even as his hands did a random tremble, "there remains everything that surrounds. There is the All. You must not look at the anemone without recollecting how it sprang from the blood of Adonis, killed while hunting."

"There *is* purity," Chappell said.

"I am pure enough, sir."

"Self-judged is self-flattered."

"No, I am the world's thus far. I am the twin of its dirt. My mind is all swans, rainbows, hydras, harps, eels, magic brews, and preposterous resurrections. The horn of plenty bellows."

Any more of that, indicating profound aversion to study, would get him into hot water: Chappell was serious, like any paralytic watching one of the able-bodied prancing by. "Rustication," he said: a raw threat, sending the young student back home for as much as an entire term, there to rethink his ways and put a veneer of humility on his cheek. Yet rustication for him would not mean return to the countryside, but to London, where he was born, son of a Catholic-turned-Protestant. Rustication, as far as he was concerned, was return to Cambridge, where they quartered the heart and made the mind a wen of dust.

And so it was. Banished to the city he came from, he felt purged and renewed, pagan again in his own mottled way, and ready for readings unprescribed and hectic. This happened to be the Lent term, the one of going without, but it was going to turn, he thought, into a feast, like going off to Nineveh undercover with only a dagger and a hard loaf to keep him safe. Or was it Persepolis? He was going to ride in triumph away from stuffy, torpid Cambridge with its Cam and its damp Chappells, its incessant east wind and its inert rivers. A jail of reeds. He longed for bustle, sunshine, crowds, a world of unkempt morals, where the will had something to cut its teeth on.

Now he was Pelops, feeling Hermes ram the ivory prosthesis into place beneath his collarbone, shrugging at him to teach him how to move the shoulder from now on, cursing Demeter, who had eaten the flesh that used to be there. She would eat herself when the fit was on her, he said. And the soupy blood streaming behind him, the young John, from where the ivory had been forced home with spikes and sap, made a carpet of anemones for his pursuers to walk upon. All the way from Cambridge to London, he dreamed himself into grandiose roles, giantkilling here, shipsinking there, tugging a vineyard from an open fold in his belly, reaching swans down from flight and blowing them up like trumpets with their beaks deep into his mouth. It was time to be different, to be new, to be dipped among the broth of stars like the poles of Earth itself. *Going home*, he whispered, away from the lean intellects, the three-legged stools, the priests in wolves' clothing. An enormous catapult slung him all the way, soaring above fields and streams, thatch roofs and coupled lovers, greasing him with magical flux, a son going home to a different kind of trouble among lewd, sweet gardeners along the musky coast of Araby.

He knew he was home in London when, having dismounted from the horse-drawn omnibus, he gave himself a good stretch and soothed his legs by raising them in turn to the top of a bollard, at which some hussy commented on the fine calves he had, calling him a fine young squire and inviting him to bed down with her for half an hour, more if he needed it. A far cry from Scholastic logic, he thought, eyeing her chapped lips, the blatant scraped-looking ruddiness of her cheeks, her general look of disrepair, through which her buxomness bulged and presented itself: a ripe orgy for the buying, at which he peered, travel-worn as he was, wondering why he had never paid the price, groped under sacking or silk, smelled alien brassy breath from the mouth of someone paid to come close to him. She had a scapegrace arrogance to her, lolling tall in front of him, her hidden flesh rippling as if she were part molten, her hands gesturing at him part by part, her not-so-clean brown hair blown this way and that in a sidespill—a carefully managed commercial flaunt, as if this were the most mobile component of her. Yet all he could think was how much he wanted to be reunited with his books at home, hug his parents, his brother and sister, and get on with his intellectual life among the Romans and the Greeks, spurning this girl's chapped face and capacious buttocks, her huge breasts, her poorly cared-for hands. He smiled, lunged, almost knocked her over, recovered and bowed, hoping she had looked away; but she had taken in all his awkwardness, told him her name was Peg, and started to laugh in a deep, jagged voice that said she had grown up on a farm or under a dray. He showed her his bookbag, opened it up as if she were a horse to feed, and she told him it would be better to have one full of breasts. Or she would empty it out, the learned tomes among the horse droppings, and clap it over his head while she had her way with his greenhorn body, making him retch and spasm, arching his back until he collapsed forward upon her. If he didn't use it, she yelled, it would fall off, so what was he waiting for. She was clean, she told him; one smell at her would prove the point, one scrape with his nail would catch no grime. He wanted to touch, but he stood frozen, jinxed by purity.

Out of *her*, he thought, the sun is pouring, the source of all brightness in this world. She has a blaze of her own, a whole jungle of delights into which prodding or poking is natural. The whole human race, bar a few prelates, had done it, so why not he? The touch or hint of dropsy only made her entire frame even more desirable as she began to stalk around him, making a lewd circle of self-display, butting her rear at him, then her bosom, then maneuvering the palms of her hands as if she were rolling dough. It was a fine, stirring show, making him want to follow her, burn his books, and devote his next twenty years to lust. He was a man, and he should prove it at least twice a week. What was the going rate? Would his father tell? Pushed beyond ordinary constraint, he advanced upon her. Here he came, gobbling air out of nervousness, and draped his hand across the double globes of her front, marveling at their sheer weight, their malleable availability. She egged him on to feel further, strident catalogue of herself, and his questing finger felt lapsing flaps or fins easily folded this way or that while she howled with laughter, telling him to tug away, so long (*slong*) as he paid for what he felt at. A long feel, he heard, sets up a young gentleman for the full day.

He could hardly bear to tell himself this was the first time he had laid hand on the organ in question, the shaggy half-pear he longed to incorporate somehow into his demure verses, in the end dubbing it "the zone." His finger smelled as if he had been grappling with an old haddock, but he prudently told himself that perhaps the smell was the crucial part, without which none of the rest would happen. Only that close to heaving up did the male feel lascivious, somewhere between loathing and voracity. She spat in his face, gave him a hard dunt with her fist right where he had been feeling hard, most Ovid-like, and then plunged an index finger right up his nose, making him squeal, his eyes run, and at last his blood run down over his mouth. "No pay, you have me not," she snapped at him. Not even a handful. It was over. He had failed again. Nothing to boast about, only yet another impromptu exercise in falling short, proving he was destined for poetry or the clergy. She stormed off in search of riper clients, her shawl and hair blown sideways by a stiff London wind, almost on the point of being detached from her body, ripped away no sooner than flung.

There was nothing for it but shame. Away dodged his imagination as, piling his books back into their bag, he called himself Orpheus, torn to pieces by drunken devotees of Bacchus. The head of Orpheus floated down the River Hebrus as far as the isle of Lesbos. His own might drift down the Thames as far as the Isle of Dogs. Greatness in those Greeks—notoriety, disgrace, true flair for sticking out like a sore finger—came from courage, not from hanging back. It was merely a matter of coming as close as possible to the event, the disaster, and then closing your mind: coaxing yourself to the brink and then fixing the mind on a certain star so as to plunge *undaunt-ably* into the abyss of scent. Was that indeed where he was going, all of him, with no hope of withdrawal? The first ever of his flashes forward came to him then as he trudged forward, gasping from the weight of his books. Someone, deep in swarthy futurity, said aloud that the best sex he ever had was in Puerto Rico, which was where the women liked it most. Perhaps an old sailor said it, an old salt looking back on a life of assiduous swiving, getting the whole world into the comparison. Where did they love to do it most? Where did they make love to their very occupation? Madagascar? Cádiz? Or the Bermoothes?

"J OHN, YOU ARE SHAKING," HIS FATHER EXCLAIMED. "WELL met, son." Now he could ask his father about the piece of you that stiffened, wobbled, then went incorrigibly erect. Mark the stern purity of that stance. Up had gone his father's yard to make him, the very son who held back, even with his finger in a wench's placket. Should he then renounce luxury by living in a tub, like—His father braying about something amiss in the house, a broken window, a chimney that puthered if the wind blew, a door that scraped. What had his own hand felt that day? Something like so-called budge, the fur used on scholars' gowns. Clipped off women of low repute, then, and stuck home with oxblood? Nothing less garish would suffice as, home at last among the soothing aromas of broth and beef, bread baking and wood crackling, he tried to keep alive the unsatisfactory lewdness of the day, with the merest speck of slime in the depths of that only too buyable fig. He was not going to sleep tonight, tense with memory. He was a cheap model of Christ, aching to give up his godhead, emptying himself of it, to become like ordinary folk. If Christ had managed it, then why not he? It was only a matter of shedding a pretense.

How could he tell the strutting strumpet, or even the mistress of his heart (who was bound to appear someday), that his mind brimmed with places or mysterious happenings that glutted his senses? He yearned for Ethiopia, the name for all Africa south of Egypt; for such as Tithonus, made immortal but not everlastingly young; for Anubis, with a jackal's head. Ethiopia was hardly the place to bed down with such creatures, and yet he felt he was primitive enough, in fits and starts, to lead the wanton life he dreamed about, even if his head also filled with crystalline spheres and whorls. By proxy he had reveled in deeds of blood, sacrificial dismemberments and magical cures. How could he tell a whore that the Styx was between her legs and that a zone of prosthetic ivory lay between his, ever on call but accustomed to mellow entreaties from literature at large? These were not the standard dubieties of the virgin man, oh no; there was something more, a contributive irrelevance that made of him—or had up to now—an absentminded womanizer, a dotard of the flesh whose eyes watered at the sight of a tender upper female arm. Confronted and challenged, he only too readily said that the Romans must have had special troubles. He had told Chappell this very thing, saying, "Sir, the Romans must have had superbly sensitive eyes or appallingly high winds. They had a verb, sir, *lippio-lippire*, which meant to have sore eyes. Imagine, sir, a whole verb devoted to that, whereas they never needed one for having an earache or what, vulgarly, young Cambridge brothelkeepers call the stone ache. I found *lippio* in Cicero's *Letters,* sir, casting about for some treasure hitherto unnoticed. How, I wonder, do we form a verb for a state of permanent excitation in the loins."

"*Tumens*, idiot," Chappell bellowed. "Spare me the need. You find it in Tacitus, Quintilian, Martial. If you look, sir. So you see, sir, nature does decay. The word remains, but the body has altered."

"Nature does not decay," John said, "but uses decay to resume itself." For once, the man made no reply but pobbled hard (worked his chops while mumbling fast), shoving right fist into left-hand palm, pestle to mortar, waiting for the scandalous youth to take his leave. He did not know, as John did, that words had to be saved whereas nature saved itself (as they thought then).

He had to face it, though, today's Peg had made deeper inroads into him than any Greek tragedy could, had entwined deep within him rosy looms and glistening corms that, one day, would drive him hellward, with his parts all botched by smegma, his nose softening at the bridge, his eyes those of a dead fish. It would come, so perhaps he was right to fend off the evil day when lust would claim and dispatch him, blinding him to all things mental, written, or poetically dreamed up. The Pegs prevailed, having the strongest artillery, even though they wore out young. He thanked God his father had moved the family from Bread Street, Cheapside, to St. Martin's-in-the-Fields, Westminster, although he hated to surrender Eleanor Cobham, who had walked barefoot from here to St. Paul's with a white sheet draped about her and a taper in her hand to do penance for indulging in witchcraft. That had been 1439. Friday Street was a fishmongers' market before even Chaucer's time. Cheapside had seen many beheadings, especially in the days of Wat Tyler and Jack Cade. In Westminster he came free in his own mind, freer to summon up the Greeks and Romans less obsessed by local color. He liked to imagine, to make present to his senses what was not there: not Peg, but the phantom perfection he called Amaryllis, the name of a shepherdess in Virgil, and a flower of Ethiopia. After all, the bumptious brothelers of Christ's College sneered at him as The Lady, perhaps on account of his fair to auburn hair and his slender build. Some had even claimed he was an albino, totally deprived of blood and unendowed with sperm, somewhat like Virgil, whom detractors called Miss Virginity. He had an oval face, dark-gray eyes, and a look of tender obtuseness aggravated by having to write papers on such subjects as these: Whether Day or Night Is the More Excellent; On the Music of the Spheres; In the Destruction of Any Substance There Can Be No Resolution into First Matter. And Learning Makes Men Happier Than Does Ignorance. And On the Platonic Idea as Understood by Aristotle. He much preferred to write on such a theme as Chastity Sharpens the Mind, closely followed by Depraved Thoughts Suppressed Make the Mind Keener.

He smiled when he thought of this, actually convinced that suffocating the mind gave it Edenic impetus whereas continual debauchery enfeebled it, although he had lately been hearing that to purge the body of lust by enacting it calmed the mind with a strange enervate peace from which clear-cut ideas soared like well-drilled doves. He was not ready for debauchery or for works of genius either. What he did instead, as so many had seen, was to wield his broadsword, raising it with an almost angelic self-righteousness and swiping about him at imaginary opponents with intent solemnity. After such exertions he looked almost pink, like a new life form raised from the depths and left gasping.

Could he sleep that night? He could not, not on back, side, or front, nor crouched, nor with his head buried at the bed's bottom like a diver into cloth. He folded his phallus double, holding it firm between his thighs, but nothing erased his mental image of Peg as she walked away, at first swiveling either leg to parade its loose-hung girth, then making her rear end wallow ever the more as she got farther away from him. She was trying to suck him along after her, eager for the climactic nip of her legs, her toes tousling the back of his hair. That was how it went, wasn't it? The whole circus amounted to not much more than peeing up the woman's backside, as certain juvenile Cambridge brothelers claimed. The more he trapped his organ between his own legs, the more it swelled and kept him from sleep, from even yawning. He had even, from these same bullies or worthies, heard talk of those called *fellaytners* or *fläteners*, men or women, whose forte was mouthing and sucking; but he did not believe it, arguing that not even trollops would do such a thing, yet nonetheless wondering why the mouth appeared such a good match for the phallus, easily as precise as the other and that other, whom the brothelers hymned in uncouth couplets learned in boarding school, where their depravities began. He wanted to be seven or eight again: untempted by what Cambridge called the hand gallop.

Alone in the pantry after dinner (the household retired early), John lit a couple of candles and looked for a dish of uneaten bread pudding: a simple enough concoction of butter, milk, and old bread. Into this he slid his hand with fingers pointed, imagining hard a Peg or just about anyone else. He sensed an alien givingness, a glide as into custard, and allowed that it was tempting, though not enough to drive men mad. His tongue soon followed, though there was not enough of a uniform depth. The sensation was erratic and incomplete, so he tugged horsehairs from the sofa and wholly disgusted himself. Disappointed too, because he had been intending to eat the leftover pudding, he found an aging custard and devoured that, wondering what in woman amounted to crust. As he squatted there on a frail box that easily bore him, he improvised as best he could, hugging loaves to him and feeling their pneumatic give and take, draping fine-sliced beef over his face before siting it lower down, giving his loins a clammy, invaded feel, and finally slapping a lump of clotted cream against his palm, then rubbing with both hands as if it were an ointment. He was approximating, with desire afoot.

This, he supposed, was how monks instructed themselves about experiences banned and denied. The heart fretted itself into a headache from overmuch imagining. How those austere, dedicated men lifted eye and hand from their latest illuminated manuscript and cozened themselves into seeing, flagrant there against the wall, Lady Philosophy or the Virgin of Untrammeled Night. Leaking from behind an exquisite loop, gold or silver sent their appetitive souls malingering. They knew that their only relief consisted in applying precious hues in such a way that either tint became the shadow of something ineffably nicer, to be guessed at or prayed to. So this was not a unicorn they embellished, but a woman's flank; and this was not the buttock of some beauteous charger but of a Peg, trolloping off to market herself. Dried-up men, they sometimes managed to seep into their coarse robes after exerting their imaginations mightily with pen or brush in hand. Perhaps they even dreamed they larded custards into the placket of some fairy queen, who lay still, curled in and out of the fringed filigree vines, while the rapt brothers illuminated. That was it, John said: they were illuminating, of course, but the illumination that mattered most came to them from elsewhere, from a source of uncontained radiance. When a monk illuminated a letter, he was bidding for some other light to wallop him, something acridly bright and not there to be pretty or soothing. You had to take your chances, like the first man or woman to lay hold of an ivory shoulder, hard and glacial where you expected flesh.

Light, which even at seventeen he thought he was being denied, was something like an explosion, either a huge fantail spilling upward into the sky, full of feathery yellows and reds, or an equally huge roiling tunnel leading nowhere yet inviting the whole human race to enter, just for the divine show. Light was chalk and lime, cuckoo-spit from the woods, a bleach of skull, and he saw all its ambiguity, not merely the conjoint light called white, but the torn and radiant hues that came together in it, quarreling until they fell into line like soldiers on parade. The universe of light was double, he told himself, thus to entice both the single-minded and the confused, especially monks, to whom the word "illumination" had overtones of initial creation. The letter was the word and the word was God. Light made you feel you were flying. It sucked you up and outward, paining the eyes to blast the mind. Again, as often in childhood, he saw Adam and Eve expelled from Paradise, on the run through a rotten and burnished cornfield, above and behind them an enormous pair of celestial nutcrackers opening to catch and rend them. The blue sky seemed full of yellow and cream blisters, cruising after the condemned pair so as to pounce, but somehow the offended light could not reach ground level, being no doubt too ethereal, and stayed swirling there, a sky's mane, fluctuating from morning to night, from white to gray. He had discovered long ago that nothing is less dark or black than the night sky, and all the talk of darkness, both punitive and shallow, was for careless lookers intent on stars only, whereas the setting was foxed or slatelike. He loved peering into the sky as into the curls that monks applied to letters, knowing as he did that new things lurked for him in mere appearances. He drank the sun whenever he could, knowing who had made it, although not in whose image.

Now, he thought, he was getting it, as when he had watched his sister sleeping, her body lax and spent like that of a loosened marionette. It would have been easy to trace the outlines of her parts and places, testing and fingering even as she heaved and churned about, her deepest dream infested by the midst-of-night incubus known as John, there not for lust but for confirmation. The female body was wounded, he could see that, and the wound never healed. Ergo there was something Christlike about all women. He had heard of seals done with thread and needle, but that was among primitive tribes in Ethiopia, say, and a civilized man knew that the only way to effect the repair was, as they said, to "take" her for the time being.

Such an act both attracted and repelled him. It seemed violent, piratical, stern, and the woman's role too passive, too much a forked surrender; not tender, mutual, so much as bumpy hydraulics. He knew better, having observed the glistening, tender exfoliations of coupling snails out under apple trees whose blossom had more than once made for him a carpet, not to lie upon but to stand upon, meditating on humankind. Talk of the burning bush made him smile; another bush burned in his mind, but mainly as something caustic and wordless: a sluice, a gash, out of which all the world had poured from the onset of time. Somehow, he felt, he was not destined to participate in that enormous service: he would not go to the pump, not even for God, although he might find himself there by accident, kneading or sniffing, a perpetual tyro. That he shrank from *cunnus* shamed him privately, but he soon drowned his shame in verbal expertise, having read all that his tutor Chappell had told him to avoid. How did it go, John's little hymnal board of the forbidden, that made him giggle and sigh?

```
cuniculosus
 cuniculus
full of rab
bits or cav
erns A rabi
bit or cony
in Catullus
in Caesar a
n undergrou
nd passage
or a mine
```

And then the master stroke: *cunnus* = *pudendum muliebre;* metonymy: a prostitute, as in Horace. Good old Horace. But the dictionaries gave only the part taken for the whole (he laughed boyishly), never the whole traced back to the part. He adored unmentionable words, half-persuading himself that "zone" was one of them, but it all depended on how you thought about the word and what venereal tropics you imagined in its hinterland. If any. He loved to think about the neuter thing of which, as the big books said, a woman ought to be ashamed. *Pudendum*, the shame part, he liked to call pudding, and *muliebre*, the woman part, mule. Hence the mule pudding that figured in his daydreams as he wondered why women should be ashamed whereas men could carry their heads high while dangling below. He was a sexual inspector, a callow but conscience-stricken observer. He was one who viewed, a voyeur before the word's time, and, being such, he felt he did not have to go further than looking. On the few occasions he felt he should, he just looked longer. Viewing the male member interested him not at all; he was attuned to shame, so-called, and what was forbidden, as in that garden.

BREAKFASTING LIGHTLY ON BREAD AND CHEESE LIKE A Dutchman, he set out to mingle among London's crowds, already an expert at feeling and fondling from behind and then slithering away at a tangent while whatever petty hue and cry raised itself up and faded out. Goosing and palming, he tested London's women from his own point of view, eager for only that transitory clutch, but amazed how deeply he could penetrate if moving at the right speed and entering at the correct angle, even with layers of wadding in his way. Whatever excitement he felt lasted only the merest time, and he felt he was more a plumber or a barber than a young lecher, telling himself it was all in the interests of science, which meant knowledge. Few women rounded upon him and swatted him in the chops for his explorations, though a good many swung at the wrong man, provoking an onslaught. As

John saw it, in the first flush of his urban rustication, a young and diffident man had to try without becoming committed. Being so surreptitious made him, he thought, quite Italian—he had heard stories of how Italian women, thus interfered with, stayed put and let the interferer have his way with them for as long as it took. Ah, the Romans again! Why had he been born here?

Cambridge's young brothelers, whom he derided in a mood of grudging envy, had taught him about the gloved ones who built up on a glove's fingers an entire repertory of groin smells, some of which lasted a season. Such gloves might be savored during an otherwise boring journey or even at dinner, extracted from one's pocket like an udder of rare spices, perhaps to be passed around the table for impromptu delectation. John had no such glove, preferring the aromas of the day insolently and haphazardly gleaned, but he reserved the right to move up in seriousness, as it were, resorting to glove or wooden figurine, comparable in urge to those who peeled an apple and kept it in their armpit for months, then bestowing it on their lover as a gift both intimate and perishable: the holy grail of perspiration. Women to men, less often the reverse. Apples absorbed, and so did pears, although pears broke up more easily under the arm's pressure. So John was a sniffer, but a tentative one, hoping one day to find an aroma so flawless he would sniff no more, except at this golden pong of the streets, fart and pheromone in one. He followed this or that woman, inhaling, guessing at the anatomy that presided, stalking perfection on all but the windiest days. London was better than

Cambridge far: it had more females to delight in.

Thought ceased as he noticed a pair of vividly painted women swaggering along in front of him: tall wenches legged like horses. He hastened forward to gain a side view and found that they were wearing elongated hooves easily a foot high, with walking slippers attached to the top. It was an old Italian fashion, designed to keep the feet dry: almost a stilt. For a moment his mind's eye summoned up maimed horses whose lower limbs had been amputated to furnish such extraordinary footgear. On a pair of these *zoccoli*, as the high shoes were known, John could have appraised the mob of London with a superior eye, picking and choosing his Pegs, and remarking en passant how Londoners, like these two whores, picked and chose their clothes from wherever they fancied, arriving at a final effect not so much international as merely miscellaneous, what with Danish codpieces, narrow Italian sleeves, and collars and doublets from France.

It soothed him to move from anatomy to what it was wrapped in. For brief moments he managed to persuade himself there was nothing beneath: no blobs, no openings, no hair, nothing of what he fantasized as lips of moist, yielding coral. Then the obsession began all over again, making him curse himself as a fondler and fingerer, hardly an authentic man. He was too much afraid of being unable to withdraw after having entered. Not only might the *cunnus* hold him fast; it might suck him in deeper, into the bowels. Or a piece of him might come off, stranded forever in the steaming interior, a

sponge for tapeworms to play with. To him there was
something grotesque about the buried phallus, sunk
deep into its destiny, whereas aloof in the rotten
air of London it had dignity and poise, clean and venti-
lated. The sulfurous pit was the last place he wanted it to
be. It did not matter. The amazing thing was that women
of all sorts and conditions, savagely opposed to being
penetrated for the deed of kind, remained complaisant
about being felt at, and up, by such as him, almost as if
manual contact from stranger or strangers completed
some facet of daily grooming. Being pawed got nobody
into trouble, did it now? So he could well envision the
rest of his career, his life, as endless testing without a
single consummation, the barbarous and frothy part of
him wholly fulfilled by fondling and dandling. A novice,
he would become a postulant; already was, but he would
never be a full-blooded anything: monk or whoremaster.
He did not want to share, but merely to borrow, a monster of abstention whose seed would always die a natural
death.

On he trod, discovering that he could say all manner of things to passersby without being of interest to
them. They at once wrote him off as a mere itinerant bab-
bler who might or might not have said "Cambridge!"
"The Lady of Christ's," or "lion's meat and the oil of red
dogs." He found this odd, as he himself doted on all he
saw and heard, like one awakened from the dead, unable
to arrive at sophistication, which he judged the state of
never being surprised by anything. Or everyone else was
indifferent, self-engrossed, intent not on attending but on

getting somewhere on time unperplexed by majestic phenomena. Did people have minds? Only as birdcages put away into a dark place and left there for casually arriving wrens to fill. Following the two whores in *zoccoli*, he increased his pace, trying to hear what they were saying, but all he heard was a muffled series of monosyllables, neither Italian nor English. Could he have happened on his first pair of whores talking Latin? Sanskrit? Seeing something that dangled, he groped forward and upward, grabbed and tugged. It came away, soft but grating in his palm, and he was off like a habitual thief, for all the world as if he had torn out a womb and was hurrying home to put it in water. What he had, almost a buttock's codpiece, was a small bag of red damask that had dangled from the belt on a stout string.

As he crouched panting in a narrow passage between another passage (barred) and a shuttered window, he opened the bag and sniffed, wondering at the complex aroma of oranges and ginger, sulfur and arsenic. What could it be? Some talisman? A keepsake? A free sample of some nosegay? The aroma seemed fresh and filthy both, bound to bring him good luck. The least it might have graced was a shoulder made of ivory. Musing thus, as much inspired by fatigue as by sheer mind, he swung the bag gently this way and that only to see it vanish and then, as the thief pounded away on long legs not worth going after, he saw his view of him break and cease as a young woman came into view from the other direction.

All that happened next was slow, and it slowed even

more as, for a second, he tried to look beyond her, seeing
her only as an obstacle. Had she really stopped? Or was
she leaning into a run? She had just crossed over and was
making a right-angled turn, but in no hurry about it. "It
was not a purse," he was going to say, but her face froze
him while his head began to throb. He knew her. He did
not. She had erupted from his memory, then, or from
Ethiopia. Not white or outright black, she was nutmeg
brown not from the sun (he could tell that) but from
birth. Her dark eyes looked almost pale next to her
matte, pulpy skin. Offering no smile, as if to recognize
with him that the thief had got a bauble not a purse, she
nonetheless motioned with her features that he had her
attention, and the briefest of nods followed. Not a move
did she make beyond that, waiting for him to seize the
initiative: move or talk, neither of which he did
—*smitten*, as colloquial dramatizers like to say, in
one instant made to grow up, deprived of all his
whimsies, his temporizings, his holdings-back.

Her face blazed through him like a loop of
white-hot ribbon, painful and narcotic, as if now he
were neither boy nor youth nor man, but some self-
transcending numinous species made of honey and
Palestinian incense. All he could think of was the word
puella, for girl, a word he had hardly ever needed. She
was the *puella* of his nights: the right hue, the right shape,
the right blend of shyness and authority. What was she
wearing? He had no idea; she was naked before him in
the street, high-busted and unhairy, with a waist severely
scooped out of the rest of her, almost as if she had been

thonged around the middle. With his two none-too-large hands he could have spanned that waist and buried his mouth in her navel. He tried to speak even as expression dwindled in her face and faded, since presumably she had nothing to say, not now she had nodded. He could not even say *puella*. He had no saliva, no breath, no traction in his lips. Had she devoured him on the spot, he would have been happier, but here he was, unprepared and helpless, browbeaten by his brown eidolon whose faintly oiled black hair took the wind and billowed, actually floated up from her skull and then gently fell back almost into place as if dying. He watched, all his brilliance and his reputation lost. If only he could— What did he want? What was this craving that had no object? Was it kiss, lick, hug, stroke, sniff, knead, or rub noses? He had no idea, able, for some preposterous reason, only to think of Apollonius Rhodius's Medea, in whom the onset of love brought on stupefying and dazzling headaches—an erotic megrim only death could cure and a dance of vengeance mitigate.

But *he* could see, though he could not be sure she was seeing him. Quite thick eyebrows. Though not joined. Thick, palatial lips endowed, he thought, with enormous stretch. Flaring, slightly flattened nose. Cheekbones a little puffed up. Chin far from stubborn, indeed soft as fungus. He groped. She was not there but a hand's breadth away, hovering, still within reach, even as he tried to keep himself from reeling backward, no more articulate than an ounce of balsam. Who? How? If only she would not hover and waver, no doubt waiting for him to identify himself, or her. Out came her hand, slight and conic, but it never reached him. He regained his balance and faced her, smiling the smile of abject infatuation, knowing she would recognize it and excuse it. He felt drunk but dry, tongue-tied and stiff-lipped, unable to cough or clear his throat, certain she found him ugly, gnarled, and awkward. He would gladly inhale her sourest morning mouth if only she would either let him go or let him soak into her, never to be seen again.

She was moving, though, during a fractional bow, a minor toss of all that hair, a volcanic hip-shrug that said, After all that I thought you were going to say something delicate to me, I am not a crude woman after all. Once upon a time she had been a phantom, that he knew, and he had brought her to life, made her into the apparition that made all other apparitions needless. He spoke, a mere blob of syllable, but it had no effect. She bloomed somehow, a touch bigger all over, and then she began to go about her business, sauntering, easy.

He willed her back, though, suddenly aware that the mere sight of her had effaced something from the heart of his being: he no longer mattered save to be her adorer, her slave, her swain. It was uncanny to feel so pendent, freed of all his Latin, his wit, his myths, and now like a berry needing the sun, nothing cleverer than that. In a sense he was praying to her and doing nothing else, yearning for her to calm him with a touch. And what he had thought was her departure, with a wave or an upflighted finger, was in fact a halt, her finger beckoning him to follow.

Should he stay, the better to marvel?

Should he follow, which he longed to do?

Should he run away, to keep her image safe in mental frost forever?

Plunging after her, who had not moved, he ran up against her softness, into the maze of the strange scent of oak about her, into her thigh. She said nothing, but tapped him on the shoulder to reassure him about time to spare and then allowed him to escort her from behind as she strode methodically, her head held superbly high, through the teeming street. I have been hooked, he told himself, I am going to my doom high on a mountain, in a refuse dump draped with sacking in a slimy cellar. Goodbye, Cambridge. What I am and have will not be sufficient for this. She, though, seemed to have no qualms, leading him like a dog, looking back every now and then to check his progress, half-beginning a wink but never going through with it. Everyone peered at him, wondering that so poor, so ungainly a youth could afford so fine a hussy, who did not so much put on airs as have them daintily obey her. He wanted to stop her, saying the walk had been enough, there was no need to go on with it. She entered a passageway, passed through a tattered curtain, no doubt an old carpet, and began to climb some stairs, entering an open doorway, descending some more stairs, after which she crouched, seemed to enter an ill-lit tunnel and then move through another doorway. He followed, puffing, wondering why she strode along with such untroubled bravura while he was all lungs and snuffle. Entered, though farther behind her than when he had started, he tried to decide what the indoor smell was:

nothing pleasant or fresh. He smelled rotting meat, cooking perhaps, but then he became aware of what hung on lines arranged across the room ("hovel" was more the word). Wet and dripping deerskins, and perhaps skins of dog and fox, dangled in the half-light, tinting the straw beneath, upon which sat cushions of various sizes, some of them blood-spattered, some of them gaping open, torn by teeth. She had pets, then, in this squalid little tannery where no cup, no dish, no blanket varied the scene, and no book, no fire. No table, no window, although he saw a square-shaped slot cut in the floor, perhaps to receive a ladder, but when he looked he saw only a wooden chute leading into darkness. She had vanished behind a long hide, but reappeared removing her outer garments, making a fanning motion to keep him at bay while she stripped off nearly everything and began to shiver. Round her she then draped a dry-looking fur and pulled it closed across her bosom and hips. Something infernal was about to begin, although her smile was abstracted, her mouth lolling expressionless.

Perhaps not, he thought. "Perhaps," he said.

"You will see," she murmured. "Being here."

"I could go now." He heard the wind in the chute.

"No," she sighed. "We need you. Who *are* you?"

"John," he said, automatic and hoarse. His hands were shaking and his eyes blinked nonstop. He was going to be murdered in a minute or so.

He sat still, hearing the distant crash of pottery, the rumble from her stomach, the advance and approach of some heavy-footed person up and down all those stairs, the cry of a descending bird of prey, a goshawk perhaps, the snuffle of some animal behind the curtain, a thud as of some headsman's ax, a baby's throttled whine, a sluice of poured water, all this as some distant paraphrast tried to combine emblems of the world, and nothing happened. She tapped her long-nailed fingers against her well-manicured teeth, shrugged lightly at him, and closed her eyes to calm her mind. All the questions in his head jostled one another so much that he asked none of them. "Oh, the smell," he said, without intending to say anything, and she suddenly reached behind her, maneuvered with both hands, and lunged at him as her bear fur opened wide, and smothered his face in a dark-smelling fruity perfume that blotted out the tanning smells and made him choke. Never mind, he had seen the big swarthy breasts with black nipples almost like puppy's muzzles and her black-flowering tuft, the fantastically constricted waist, the ripe billowing curve of her buttocks.

What was she waiting for? Was he supposed to fling himself upon her and try to pee up her backside? Was he supposed to break into tears and plead? Was he supposed to strip and then grovel near her lap? She was shaking her head, deploring his lack of savoir-faire, but leaning toward him, reaching into his codpiece, lifting his midriff against her bosom, and like a maniac with a dead strawberry, gently then harshly pressing one of her huge nipples into the little slit in his glans. She held him there, suckling, until there began a tremendous thumping on the stairs, louder for descending, and in burst a huge bearded man wearing a kilt, on his head some kind of naval hat. Without so much as looking at John, he tumbled him away from her and heaved into place. Now John understood that he was the required watcher, the one without whom they would feel less excited, though whether they had in mind someone as appalled and sickened he could not tell.

In the main she kept silent, but the bearded sailor (or whatever) let out guffaws, roars, spittle-thick sighs, brays, raves, and uncouth foreign words as he pummeled and barged her, ending sitting on her throat with his enormous belly before her face, in threat, bribe, or reward. Stunned John could not tell. It was not, he thought, as if he had asked for this display, or been invited, or paid. Forced on him thus, it seemed unsexual, more of assault and battery than lustful, but, oddly, the lascivious union did not make her seem less exquisite than he had thought her at first. Somehow the coarser her behavior, the suaver she seemed, clearly a woman of delicate sensibility capable of transmuting lust's onset into something demure and fine: a storm raging through her body but becoming civilized en passant. Something like that. She was a shuttle or a loom weaving coarse yarn. Indeed she made no grunts or gasps, but let the bearded man make of her what he would, finding her paralyzed with delight by his ardor, or assuming an indifference his ardor would not heed. John made no move to interfere or somehow to take part, just vaguely aware that he was witnessing something in the genus *orgy*, commonplace rather than outrageous. She had brought him here to see, no doubt having seen the bemused, idealizing look in his eyes, wanting to shake it out of him while the sting of her nipple in his glans made him feel deflowered, yet oddly singled out, recognized as special. It had never occurred to him that, among all the bizarre combinings of sex as he knew it from the Cambridge brothelers, such a thing could be, still less be an occasion of pleasure. To him it seemed bad style, a poor juxtaposition, and lacking in the very originality it pretended to. My goodness, he thought, if they do that, they attempt other perverse combinations as well, like Master Shakespeare. Still and all, the list of possible combinations must surely be small, which must frustrate the most active lovers of both sexes. Within a year all the variants would be worn out, would they not, and folk would be hard put to it to startle their partners with uncanny grips, terrible presentations, unheard-of twists. With more apertures and more protuberances, he thought, the game would be more provoking; otherwise, translating Latin, or writing in it, like a leftover show-off, would be more fun. Less procreative to be sure, but more like gossamer, like debate, like writing. Whatever her name was, and he thought Amaryllis as good as any, his mind on the nut-brown shepherdess in Virgil, she gave the kilted sailor his due, toppling him off her not a moment too soon, emerging from their encounter with a face of attenuated exasperation. Clearly she did it for money.

HE WAS WONDERING ABOUT THE ONGOINGNESS OF life. Should there always be something that happened next or, at some juncture, should the whole thing stop? Was life more of a series of waits than a rapid succession of tingling events? Which would be preferable? He had no time to wonder more, as life choked back his question. Amaryllis began to sing while standing, a sound of excruciating pain, staccato and undulant, a sustained cry not addressed to anyone in particular but cast into the air, left to carry to wherever it would. It was a howl that nothing would appease, he could tell that, and it almost seemed to invite the sealing up of the mouth. Perhaps it was a plea for just that: a broken heart drove the ruined larynx, and the tongue fluttered at speed in an almost Arab yell that John could not identify. He linked it mentally with charging tribesmen in Ethiopia and, for lack of response, tried to do it himself, copying its agitated crescendo, but his mouth was dry, his lips had become rigid. Amaryllis went on with her yell while the figure in the kilt stood up, reeled, and withdrew, but not before John glimpsed the absence at the groin of the usual male luggage. Had this been a woman with a beard? If so, what in fact had the pair done in front of him? He tried to ask, but all she did was come nearer and bellow her acrid, grievous yell into his face. Perhaps it was the battle cry of rotting skins. Now she grabbed him by the loins, but he shrank and shrank and soon the wincing acorn of his sex had almost vanished into his body cavity. He got the weird impression that she thought her song, by pounding his nerves, would make him stiffen up. Failing to provoke him, she seized his head and made as if to suckle him, an activity he preferred and began to enjoy, hoping that the other person or creature would not return. At least, she had stopped singing now, settling for a coarse croon that began to soothe him, though his nose was blocked and his mouth felt frayed and numb. So long as she did something to him, she did not seem to care. Up she got and made water into a wooden pail behind the skins. Returning with an apple that she cracked in half with firm and agile hands, she shoved a piece into his mouth and motioned to him to eat. He chewed and swallowed, at which point she gave him suck again, now and then giving his privates a sharp flick of her middle finger, roaming around his loins with predatory thoroughness.

John felt as if he had never had any other life. What had just happened in here seemed to have wiped out everything else: home, Cambridge, languages, even Peg and the bag of red damask he had snatched from the whores tottering on *zoccoli*. Even as he sucked he groped for it, half intending to give it to Amaryllis as a gift. He had forgotten: it was gone; but he no sooner missed it than she produced it, recovered by her lover of a moment ago, as if he read minds and, while feeding his lust, also dealt in stolen goods.

"Against the plague, my lad," she said with systematic brashness. "Plenty in there. Arsenic, sulfur, carnations, nutmeg, myrrh, radish leaves, gingerroot of course, orange peel, mastic, rue seeds, and peony leaves. All mixed together. It hangs about the neck, over the heart. You must be careful not to sweat against it. I call it a badness bag, but you will hear people calling it other names. Here, see what I do with it." She opened her thighs, took the bag from him and pushed it out of sight. "Thank you," she said, with the sigh of one sitting down after a long stand. "I'll rest easy now."

She told him her name, but he knew an Amaryllis when he saw one; she told him where she came from and explained how many African and Arab strains mingled in her being, but he summed all that up as Ethiopic, otherwise known as blackamoor. Amid all those potential leathers she smelled of peppermint, which she chewed and then spat out, replenishing her wad from a pocket he could not see. She refreshed him. She terrified him. She appealed to the exotic side of his mind, bringing a dream home when he least expected it. He saw she was bleeding from where she had put the damask sack, but all she did was dip her finger and paint a red line down his nose, as if applying warpaint. "Women, my young pretty," she told him, "are of mysteries choke-full. They would not be women if they were not. You are here to see, and now you have seen."

This was how she made a living then. He wanted to rush back to Cambridge and tell the brothelers all he had done, but as he made to move she tugged him back, which made him swell, and then she took him in her mouth, mumbling as she did so and cuffing him again to keep him stirred. John had spilled his seed before, but not like this; and now he waited to be asked to pay, but she said nothing, only forcing her mouth upon his in an educative kiss that made him splutter and await a biblical hammer that would fall from the roof and split his head like an egg. This was like doing several years at Cambridge in an afternoon; and, lacking anything else to do, she had soon tweaked and probed his all, instructing him to make the girls he knew do these things to him, and he began to glimpse the monster he was going to be, demolishing old rigmaroles and uncovering his friends to themselves, revealing the unknown to them even as they grew up, gasping and hedging. In a trice, John would have become the learned man of his group, their *real* tutor, not only teaching them that *sperm whale* was a misnomer, from a mistaken idea of what spermaceti was, but why real sperm was called spunk, from the fungus that grew on trees.

All taught him by Amaryllis. He could concoct anything and attribute it to her. All very well, except he was

not that outgoing a youth, and he was likely to keep such
matters to himself for verses or letters, even for private
charms recited at night as demons woke up and began to
roam. She was eyeing him now with affectionate acerbity.
It had always been her custom, she explained, to bring
young men here, to watch or to do, she was tired of older
clients, and besides, she was not an unlettered woman
(though she gave no proof). Had he actually sucked
blood from her nipples? Silly, she said, but she knew
where blood was in good supply, nearby and private. He
demurred, but put his head back on her bosom while she
felt at him all over, teasing him with such rigor that he
became inflamed as never before and allowed her to
move his mouth about her body, now tasting beetroot,
now copper, as she directed him and rammed him about,
devastating his old idea of anatomy gained from some
younger than him.

At ease with peculiar acts, he began to chuckle, not
so much at being rudely initiated as at the peace he had
found in this hovel, where nothing was forbidden, and an
athletic sow might trot out from behind a goatskin to join
them on the floor in a long bout of mixed company. As
decorum died, so did his idea of woman as a paragon. He
wanted to shout, to squirm. He did. Out of Amaryllis
came a kind of parsed fire, not to burn him but to coax
his nerves and muscles, prompting him to catch up with
himself. The only trouble was that she had clients, other
clients, and would no doubt pass on from him to other
greenhorns. How would he ever find her again? He
would come back with repeat energy, but she would have

to want him. Should he offer her some poetry? How many lines would it take? She was not unlettered, as she had told him, but her Latin would be limited. Would she even care if day or night was more excellent? Did she think that nature was subject to old age? Had she ever pondered the music of the spheres? He did not dare to ask, telling himself that only the sow thistles and brambles of Cambridge accompanied such asinine thought. The grayfly and a mongrel deity.

Had the rest of the world blown away, with his friends King and Diodati, Anne his sister and Christopher his brother? Was there a way back to the world he knew, up the steps first and then down the others? Would he henceforth see with different eyes? Would some dreadful pox follow him and strike him down, like powder in the blood? A worm could grow in his brain, stifling all grammar, or into his ear, cutting him off from music. What was there now to look forward to at twenty-one, thirty even? Forging ahead, never mind in how awkward and helpless a way, he had forestalled futurity. The even crescendo of days, verging from a march into a process, was no longer his. He was into Virgil, having skipped Caesar, and he was never going to forgive himself. God was bound to intervene and punish him for anticipating so much. Into his bodily system, kept trim with broadsword and cold water, would come a blight, retarding him and stunting his growth, some ailment so gross that he would at once know what it was for and why it had come. Now he wanted to take back, subtract, the callow delights of his day in strange company, but they were his forever: the sleek and sharp contraband of pain.

Whatever magic carpet of filth and horror he was riding, he wanted to be off it, but away she went, babbling about Italy and venomous atoms, about locking everything near and dear to her in one room and then leaving it forever so as to preserve it, wandering for months with military deserters. The plague, whatever she meant by that, lay dormant in bales of wool, old pairs of sleeves bought second hand, in the pockets of officers who gambled their soldiers' wages. Once embarked, she could not be stopped, but in a fervent rush told of death sentences for looting, mass graves fenced in to keep ravenous stray dogs at bay. Some folk had gone completely mad and claimed to have made dough from flour unburned at the burial sites; cooked in a wineless meat broth, such bread had already healed hundreds, including many members of the nobility. First, she had dressed as a monk, and then as a short, redhaired fat man with all of his possessions in a small shining box. She had lived in caves, in the huts of lumberjacks, shepherds and coal miners, terrified by a little blister the size of a coin inside her left knee, afraid to wear a bandage lest someone see her removing and reapplying it and denounce her as infected. Was that at Madonna di Monsommano? She could hardly remember: the names of places had merged, like scabs taking over the surface of the skin. Then she became a gold beater from Palermo, tall and thin, with a Nazarene hat and walnut hair. In the agony of her mind's eye she rang the changes endlessly on her appearance and vocation. One maniac she traveled with, no doubt in a circle, had already poisoned holy water in several cities. For him she carried a bag that contained vegetable oil from Volterra, soil from Empoli, pilaster scrapings from Ripomarance, for toothaches, and alum used for cleaning ice.

Later, she posed as a street vendor of pins and needles, ever on the run from the plague and the authorities, the logic of those times having been that anyone who moved was suspect and had to be strung up by the arms to an apple tree and tortured from below. Usually, she said, the agony of having your arms tugged out of their sockets was enough to make you confess that you were indeed a spreader of the plague: either you had come from where it was or you knew where it was going to be because you took it with you. In one town, perhaps Leghorn, she and her associates were rounded up and shoved into a dungeon for trying to impersonate characters in novels: wandering around aimlessly, cheating the poor and aping the well-to-do, pretending to know the meaning of life and what other people were thinking. One of her fellow travelers had a black-and-white beard, like graphite next to snow, and she wondered if he stained it or had merely worried with one half of his mind, while staying serene with the other. She had hidden herself in a field of lupines paler than periwinkle but bluer than zenith, worked with a spade in vineyards, and, disguised as a man, had even become an infantryman in the army of the prince of Satriano, who was fighting for Genoa against Savoy. It did not matter. The main thing was never to be stationary, even if going in a circle the other way around. When buboes appeared on people's elbows or between their legs, they began to scream.

No, she told him, she had said it wrongly: those who moved about were arrested as potential carriers of the plague—*pestifera vagationis*—while those who stayed put were also arrested, suspected of being too ill to travel. Either way, you were wrong, and soon the police began to be arrested by the populace, but no one wanted to lay hands on anyone else. The only sufferers who won any degree of respect were the tarantulated, bitten by a tarantula, and the wounded returning from the battle front, with all manner of faked wounds and atrocious, improvisatory limps that ceased the instant they left town. Wherever she went she came across people touting grain oil, sealed soil, and the roots of Saint Apollonia: good for fevers, good for plague. Eight armlengths was the preferred distance to keep people at, although one quack she met, Quiescan di Garbo, made it ten with, ritually laid out in a line on the ground from the end of the eighth to the brink of the tenth, some onions, a few freshwater fish, figs, bread, and cheese, to remind the plaguestricken of happier days. "They will run toward you only as far as there is food on the ground," he told her. He also theorized about water, usually after sticking a twig down his throat to induce vomiting; water from pure soil, he said, and hills that face eastward was better than water from rocky beds and hills facing north. Lead aqueducts were lethal, he claimed.

"You are not telling it straight," John complained. "I am losing the thread."

"When you are going mad, running from the plague," she said, "from where they said the plague was not, there is no thread, my pet." On she stormed, raving about the noble and the ignoble organs: heart, brain, arms, legs, as distinct from liver, kidney, bladder, lungs. Glands, she said, were always weak, and in the grand caravanserai of metaphor that all the world was, the poor were like ignoble organs, they were the race's offal. She was none of that, but an infected woman of high station condemned to roam Italy and other countries with only a buffalo coat to her name, leaving her newborn babies where they dropped, committed wholly to the impulsion to move on, to outrace the thundering plague that came behind her.

John flinched, compiling an overture to life from a stranger's harum-scarum coda. All she could talk about now was cloudy urine, wounds, chest pains, and uneven heartbeats, and buboes, buboes, buboes, black, yellow, green, or red, best isolated from the heart with tourniquets, their growth best speeded up with unguents sometimes called *rottori*, or breakers. Your standard *rottoro* was mixed as follows: mustard, poison ivy, rock salt, cantharide powder, crushed glass, turpentine, animal excrement, an onion, and pork fat. To be applied hot until the afflicted person fainted. Almond oil and lily oil had their uses too, best mixed and boiled with bran flakes and fat figs. It was best, she said, to purge the body first, and if possible through the pores, which, in angry people, were open.

"I am getting nothing," John complained.

"Whose life am I saving," she said, "mine or yours?"

"One or the other, then." In Florence, she said, it was common to burn children on the neck. That helped. The best way, though, was to administer the so-called "fountain" between the legs, cutting with a razor blade below the bubo, sucking out the blood, then applying three leeches and smothering the wound with a pigeon whose breast had been sliced open—or a plucked rooster with its soapy, gray extracts laid bare.

Since the plague began, she said, more animals than ever had been quartered: dogs, pigs, roosters, of course. The bubo had to be burned gently with incandescent gold, silver, or iron, the tool being round at the top and shaped like a diamond at the bottom. "Then bandage with cabbage leaves," she said, triumphant and breath-less, white slime in the corners of her eyes, and her nose dribbling. Snake meat, he heard, arsenic crystals, and theriaca. The snake meat had best come from an eggless female.

"Of course," he said. It was as if, against the bubo, all the rest of the world's commodities had been arrayed, as if everything that was had medical properties, human bone and blood included, and lion's meat especially. The bubo stood not a chance against the not-bubo. Why, then, all the panic? Per se the black, ashen scabs were as nothing, nor the nail-like bottom. No, she said, the true plague within the plague is the corps of barber-surgeons, who carve recklessly and sit only at the bedsides of the rich; the poor they tell to light a candle and undress. Oil of white lilies and filthy wool was their standard remedy, along with bloodletting and laxatives. They liked things to pour, she yelled. They cut and cut, then cauterize with an iron that left a purple scar. It was a kind of trademark or signature, she told him loudly. She had begun quietly, but only toward a crescendo, once again beginning a falsetto rave about salve and chicory water, young boys buried in shallow graves bleeding and bubbling, petechiae and juleps.

"How did you survive?" He hesitated to call her Amaryllis even now.

Frowning, she seemed unwilling to answer, but said suddenly as if announcing the solution of a puzzle, "The bubo's gigantic protrusion made it seem like a pregnancy. If you thought of it as one, with the right degree of prophetic tenderness, you had one chance in ten of coming through. Those who, like Paolo Bosi's wife, tried to cauterize themselves died, like those who used maltha." John was thinking of what he would tell Diodati and King when he saw them next, both still away at university, the former at Oxford, the latter at Cambridge, and how to remember all that Amaryllis had told him with her naked mind.

ALL HE COULD THINK OF IN COMPLEMENTARY RIPOSTE was the torch of white hawthorn, signifying both joy and pain; a certain giant with a hundred arms; someone who was changed into a flower when he died infatuated with his own reflection; the female monster who turned all who looked at her into stone; the driver of the sun's chariot who was hurled down into the River Eridanus for endangering Earth; and the sacred chest of Osiris carried by black-robed priests into a temple to the tune of tambourines. A beginning, he thought, to show her that I come from somewhere of equal caliber. All she has told me may be serious, consequential, but what I tell her brings the muted commotion of long, long ago, now made magical by distance, by the strange blur of hero worship. Nothing was trivial then, as at Cambridge; all was resonant and extraordinary. It took a hundred-headed serpent to kill Osiris, so scattering truth to all points of the compass, as we say. It must have been so demanding to live then, with so many gods and gods' hangers-on intimately involved in the everyday stuff of your life, although there were exceptions—only those without sin might hear the silver chime of sirens as they journeyed about the Earth, each uttering a single tone. How could anyone live without hearing the music of the spheres? Plague was one thing, but being deaf to the harmony of Creation was worse. He told her this, knowing she was more literate than she pretended to be, half-wondering in his new access of boundless primal feeling if she too might be a siren, emitting some coarser chime well short of crystalline, here to test and tempt him, waiting to see what fantastic stories he would tell her in retort.

"Tell me something else from your fabulous world. The plague has made me dither. My mind shakes about, asking for Quiescan di Garbo and all the others. I am not where I belong." Halcyons, he told her, requiring no more invitation, bred only when the sea was calm; otherwise known as the kingfisher, really Christ. Female gods, angry with male gods who had fallen in love with mortals, tried to persuade the male gods to visit their earthly loved ones, knowing the visit amounted to being struck by lightning. "I like that," she said. "That appeals. I could do the same." There was one, he said, who asked to be turned into a laurel, and was. The leaves on her tree became the symbol of Apollo's devotion to music and poetry.

"Your best only," she told him. "*That* sounds truly

weak-kneed to me. A woman should not back away like that." He sighed and tried to recall something staggering, not so much hammered home at St. Paul's School as voluptuously received as it sidled into his only-too-willing mind. "Once upon a time," he said after a deep breath, "two giants tried to overthrow the gods, and they stood one mountain on top of another one, Mt. Pelion on Mt. Ossa. What they did became a figure of speech. More interesting, though, is the coachman Thomas Hobson, who drives between Cambridge and the Bull Inn in Bishopsgate Street, here in London. Another figure of speech, 'Hobson's choice,' came into being because any customer wishing to rent a horse had to take the one nearest the door or go without. He was the postman who carried pleas for money from Cambridge to London and refusals the other way—mostly. A man in constant motion, one of our most convenient lions."

"This Hobson," she said friskily, "knows his own mind. One day, soon, the plague will oblige him to seek other employment. No more weekly trips."

"Yes," young John said suavely, "all that happens is a mere approximation or reflection of some purer happening. We are shadows among shadows, obliged to guess, as we do in poetry and plays. Now, let me see. Someone you would not know was killed by a boar while hunting. He bled to death, but the anemone sprang from his blood. One of my favorite ones. Someone else"—he knew now that he was scraping away at the bottom of his barrel—"cut into pieces as food for the gods, was put back together, but a chunk of his shoulder had already been devoured, so they replaced it with ivory. That is one of my most favorite ones, madam. I see the Greek sun striking it like a piece of cuttlefish bone, and the reflected light browning the neighbor flesh, which only further accents the white of the implanted part." He could feel his mind wanning, his heart fainting, his eyes getting bleary. He wanted to go on talking with this female, but he was too weak from sexual exertion, such as it had been, and listening or talking. He told her he was hungry, and out she fished a bowl of congealed soup with a buff-colored lid of dripping on top, stirred it with her forefinger, thus breaking up the dripping, and handed it to him, then an encrusted wooden spoon. One retch or two later, he began to scoop and chew, wishing himself far away, in Hobson's coach or one of the inns en route. The dripping was like tallow, the soup like dishwater, but he persisted, holding his breath in between spoonfuls. I am not who I am, he told himself, I am the ghost of my superior: the crystalline John, whose true nature may only be guessed at. I am given to melodramatic turns of phrase. The only true alchemist is the sun. Our exhalations drift away from us to up on high, where they become moon spots. "Cambalu, Oxus," he told her, "Agra and Lahore, Chersonese and Ecbatana: all places I dream upon, hoping one day to travel there. I read all night, memorizing, and then I have to have rue and euphrasy, to cleanse my eyes."

"You wish," she said. "What do you wish most?"

"To have the seals removed from my eyes."

"Other than medically."

"To become a poet of mountainous gift."

"Pelion piled on Ossa?"

"Upon Helicon, madam."

"Why 'madam'?"

"Well brought up by a scrivener, which—"

"I know, John. Are you seeing the true me or the approximation, then?"

"You know. Do they read Plato in Italy?"

"I am not Italian but Ethiopic, Arabian, an unintimidated wanderer, dark from my ancestors. White teeth from contrast. Dark frizzy hair. An aroma like that of truffles scented by flies, then dogs and pigs. Be good to me and I will be your muse."

Now he was Atahualpa the Inca king, or the Khan of Mongolia, Nimrod the founder of Babylon. She was yawning. "How did you like my soup?"

All he could do about the soup was nod. No one, he knew, any longer could remember what was in it: no unicorns, anyway, no harps. So, it was her unicornless, harpless soup, more a category than a flavor. Was there no heat in here? He asked. She stuck the bowl between her legs and covered it with a shawl. Actually, she was domesticating him, in a perverse tradition, of course, but nonetheless raising him from the level he had been at, readying him for the whirlpool, the plague. He asked for Quiescan di Garbo, only to be told that he had just left. "Gelded he came, gelded he left," she said, "but he likes to go through the motions, like an armless oarsman. It was done to him in Italy when they suspected him of carrying the plague. He goes out and scrambles for food.

61

Smells like a fishmonger, but he saves me daily."

"From?" He trembled, wooden spoon in hand awaiting the warmed-up bowl.

"From boredom. From the agitations of a scarred memory, from the familiar predicament of someone who, trying to forget elephants walking afire, remembers them all the more keenly."

"Ah." He sighed, quoting from himself in a language he thought she knew. "Ah quoties dignae stupui miracula formae quae posset senium vel reparare Iovis! Ah, how many gorgeous arses—"

"You liked them that much?"

"Shamefully. I love the flesh."

"You know nothing about it."

"But I am licking my lips, madam."

"Muse."

"Muse, then."

"Why prate of worn-out Jove, worn out in bed, when you have not even tasted the joys of first frenzy? You're guessing again, John. I was your first, was I not? Am I not? Not just your first black hussy but your first hussy, your one and only puss?"

He reached over and took the bowl from where it sat, scooped into it again, and smeared the half-curdled dripping over his mouth, smacking his lips. He had begun growing old. A facetious thought, perhaps, but he sensed it was impossible to have an identity when your body, your soul, were ever on the move: dwindling, swelling, molting, sprouting. Humans felt obliged to pretend to consistent self, which was never more than a bundle of mutable qualities: rather like someone taking a compass direction for a planet.

How the mind chatters to itself, he thought—what in the north they call chunter. Most of what we say reflects little of this chatter-chunter and becomes as a hoard of indistinguishable sunsets, all of them watched developing with the full gradient of emotion, but then lost, even the unique ones. How can one know anyone, or even oneself, without in some way taking account of the undersea iceberg? Human relationships thrived on the surface, shallow and skimped. Every human, he thought, needed a poet to speak for him, and a different one. Certainly, the great poets spoke for all human beings, but not so often of the inland commotion that as accurately defined someone as all their utterances did. With Diodati and King he had done some plumbing, and they with him, which meant they thrived in a profound reciprocity fine enough when phrased like that, in Latinate words, but not so splendid when called, oh, deep friendliness. It was not the Romans but the Germans who evolved the cult of the sister's son. He had learned this from books. He suspected that nearly all the deep bonds among friends, since time began, fulfilled themselves only fractionally, since human beings had enormous trouble with one another's privacies. To write well, as he intended to, one had to grow antennae and steer them in deeply until, glory be, the human subject began to emerge in something close to ravishing completeness, all the sluices of the mind emptied, the granary of memory ransacked, all half-completed thoughts fleshed out, all severed utter-

ances drawn into the open and combed until they were
linear, whole. To do this for even a few would be the epit-
ome of neighborly epiphany. He smiled at how easily
words came about the ease with which words did not
come. How easily he prated to himself about difficulty.

Amaryllis, about whose mouth he noted the tiniest
crystals in a crescent line (sugar or powdered glass), was
asleep, hunched forward in an alert doze. He and she had
exchanged histories and myths, but neither had learned
much about the other, even during the raw and perfunc-
tory clips they had exchanged. In the end, he suspected,
human pairs made the best of the little they knew about
each other, each working on the basis of the other's
guesswork, but to a huge befuddlement sooner or later.
Woe to the self-describing subject, he exclaimed mentally.
In a profound sense we are unknowable, and our lives are
shielded, like the trilobite that has three main parts: the
part that holds the head, shielded; the middle, composed
of pieces distinct from one another and unjoined; and
the tail, which also has distinct pieces, but linked, as
if diffidence had died a natural death and kindred bits
combined.

One day, he thought, there would be urns that
enclosed the entirety of a human's thoughts over a lifetime. A man might delve therein to find out what he had
been thinking, without knowing it, when he made his
first sandcastle or caught his first fish. John would not see
it, he knew, but he wished for it almost as much as he
longed for the Second Coming, which would make reli-
gion magical all over again, less a fetish predicated on a

dry guess. He was going to tell Amaryllis these things, to be told in return more about Italian plague-mongering, if indeed it had been Italy she had come from, and not Egypt or Arabia.

How readily he and she slid sideways out of their diurnal roles, skimping repetitious ephemera and casting their lives, or the lives of others, in a higher reach: aggrandizing, perfecting, dramatizing, as if ordinary human lives were not worth talking about, but only magic bonnets on plague victims, appalling stenches from heaped cadavers turning into wonderful fragrances to breathe which was to be cured, roselike and celestial. Or if not that, gleaned from Amaryllis's babblings, professional mourners who turn into nymphs who then change into (to name one or two) a lotus tree, a poplar tree, and a goddess of flowers. He doted on these Hyades, the daughters of rain. Or consider the case of Cassiopeia, he thought, boasting that her daughter Andromeda was more beautiful than the Nereids; for that, Andromeda became a constellation. As if at grammar school, he imagined the imaginary punishment: the tutor saying "Cassiopeia, go and stand outside, and become a constellation." Wondrous! What was this urge, then, to embellish, as if life were never enough, as if history were one long disappointment? Was it to make at least something unforgettable, recovering it from the putrid monotony of history? He thought he understood, being himself a natural maker of myth, wanting not so much to reproduce God's handiwork as to copy God's habits with God's ready-made material. Something like that tugged at his mind and made it want to alchemize the *quidditas*, the whatness, of amassed experience—deifying humans, humanizing gods, devising (as the Greeks had) the force that tells the gods themselves what to do, like a cosmic manager. A Hobson of heaven imposing his will on all comers.

So this, he decided, was the disappointment on which all great religions based themselves. Was it not Buddhism through which there ran a perpetual even if well-domesticated strain of disappointment? Life in God's universe could have been better, if better designed. He had heard these arguments or complaints from himself before, having no idea that, centuries hence, learned conjurers were going to write books about his notion of God, just as they were going to confect books about Shakespeare's doctrine of nature in *King Lear*. This was only the beginning for him. He was a lad theologizing, so intent upon his vision and successive renderings of it that he found himself unable to write letters, least of all in Latin or Italian. Each time he tried, his mind reeled away, as from bloodshed, and he contented himself with the near-mercenary thought that his friends would forgive him, knowing he had better things to do. He did now and then write letters, but his mind aimed upward, at and past the stars.

"You slept," he told her as she yawned and did a rapid shrug.

"Or the world slept while I waked." He had heard this line before, mostly in the form of when you die the universe dies with you.

He was brooding on the plague. "It is coming, you say. We are not ready."

"Nobody ever is," she said, scratching at her calves. "People never believe it, and then they have to start burning bodies."

She sounded so experienced, so versed in human daftness, that he asked her age, only to be slapped down. "Old as this strawberry nipple, boy. Let that be your answer."

Not even scatomancy would solve this problem, so he told himself she was nineteen, though she was ten years older—soft-complexioned, though, with a strong tide of blood coursing through her. Was she still wearing the damask bag where she put it?

"You are really him now," she cooed.

"I am him? Grammar forbids—"

"A man. God's blood, a *man*."

"Just like that."

"Certainly not from removing wax from my ear."

"How uncouth."

"And unnecessary. Was it not Icarus who flew so near the sun the wax in his ears melted?"

Cackling, John envisioned the scene: the young aviator pawing at his ears as he fell toward a rind of blood-red sealing wax. "This Quiescan di Garbo," he began, "will be back?"

"In his time a famous scholar, John, whom you should emulate. Much more learned than I, although I myself am no little bag of dung. Despite my sufferings and my wanderings, I have turned to thought as other women turn to kneading dough."

He believed her, but not her stories of the plague. He suspected her of a movable plague designed to win interest and exploit sympathy. In that event, however, she was a born tale-spinner, full of happenings as an ox of suet. Now he tried to get her going again.

Y ET, MEANING TO PROMPT AND PROVOKE HER, he ended up talking in his own right, explaining how he felt about things writ large: heroes depicted as braver than they were, handsome people made unendurably beautiful, exceptional feats of thought and creativity ennobled beyond belief (and beyond criticism, too). The desire to live in a perfect world exalted him even as it sometimes seemed no more than a bit of ragged burnt paper wafted on the winds of what the medieval poets had called "aventure or cas." To have been born into an imperfect world seemed almost a waste of promise, of hope; it was not, after all, as if the world kept getting better and better instead of accruing a longer and longer list of woes. Why should humans, he asked her, continually plague themselves with the image of perfection without ever being able to achieve it? Why should they be able to imagine any such thing? An unattainable grail, he went on, stuns the heart. We die thwarted.

Then she responded, almost seeming to creak as she spoke, dragged from some trance. "On the other hand," she said with earnest drive, "without the lure of an impracticable affection, humans would never even try. They would never begin. We regard such an ideal as a goad rather than as a goal. How wasteful that sounds, calling upon a celestial carrot to make an awkward donkey budge, but that seems to be it. Inspiring ourselves with a wholly attainable goal would never be enough."

Now he saw Quiescan di Garbo peeping at them from behind one of the hides, his eyes almost sealed, his hands fused on his chest. He seemed the worse for wear, with his kilt torn and his bare legs thick with mud. He could have been in the river or the gutter.

"Oh, him," she said, as if reading John's mind. "A receiver of punishment, I am sorry to say. He seems to attract roaring boys. Something hangdog in his demeanor draws them to him. Or indeed civilized people, eager to take out their anger on just about anybody, always seem to find him. So he lives in a storm of curses and punches. He is as often in the Thames as not. Perhaps he revels in punishment, perhaps he longs to take it upon himself. If he takes it, someone else is spared. I doubt his reasoning, but on he goes. With me he enacts his past glories, his prowess. I call him a plague target, the volunteer omnivore. Someone has to make sense of him, you see. It would be intolerable if he were meaningless."

Rather moved by this unusual speech, John felt

unable to reply, convinced that the starting point for all responses to life was the individual's sense of having one and only one chance at living: something precious, changeable, unique, almost at one's own disposal, not to be squandered, and this was the sense that drove people mad whenever they did something poorly, settled for a mediocre choice. Then, when their lives were almost over, they cried out: this was not the life we meant to have. It came out all wrong. Poor people, he thought, fair fields full of them. They never know who they are, or what will at last cut them down. No whence, no whither, and, in between, only barely defiable incertitude. They improvise, determined to do something but having no idea what to do next, and they go down bleeding, foam on their lips along with the elegiac murmur:It could have been nicer than this. Hence myth, by which we persuade ourselves that at least some of us lived the right life. A life is so much putty, kneaded and at last hardened into the shapes put into it by improvisatory abandon. My, what a serious young man I am today. Amaryllis, he was now convinced, was some metaphysical emissary: not an angel, not quite, but what he would call one of God's catastrophic monitors (those who advise), invested thickly with human daub and garb, a divine machine aimed for now at him, capable of wondrous deviation. This was why he had been rusticated, which amounted to being sent from one tutor to another, not so much from Cambridge to London as from whimsical obduracy (Chappell) to—He hovered, paused, stammered in his mind's ear.

What summed up Amaryllis? Certainly not shepherdess, worth half an hour's dalliance in Virgil's
Eclogues. What had she said her real name was? Dahlia?
Another flower. Well, something like that. She was the
wholly adaptable dominie, Fellow of Heartbreak College,
Cambridge. If she looked Ethiopic, that was a mere whim
on the part of the master of ceremonies; she might have
been, might become, as bleached and epicene as
Boethius's Lady Philosophy, who visited him while he
awaited execution.

"So pensive, so young," she whispered at him.
"Come here. We have not that much time together. The
strain is too great. I want to show you Quiescan's
wound."

He could manage without seeing the wound, he told
her; his life would not be complete, but what of that?
Was she trying to impress him with some quotation from
Boethius? She seemed to have forgotten that he was destined for the clergy, or that was what everyone, including
his father, thought. Yet John was not that obedient a soul;
too much a lover of myth to settle for daily formulas, the
orthodox round, he was as willing to tamper with
Christian history as with Greek myth. He was a maker
already, he knew, not a singer or even much of a prayer,
but one who heard long strophes in his head and dedicated them at large, sand in a whirlwind, as the mood
seized him. To be a poet, he thought, is to lose much else.

Again she mentioned the wound, and this time
Quiescan moved toward them from behind the hide,
breathing heavily and beating one palm against his

breast. Then he was on his back, groaning, his legs flailing, the kilt rutched back to his belly. John saw the peduncle, white as ash, rough-cut and gross, but most of all he saw the lack of manhood flowing out of the blister and the scar. No wonder the poor devil groaned, no wonder he tried in frantic clasps to summon up the lover he had been. The gruesome finality of his amputation made John feel queasy, but not as queasy as when Amaryllis grabbed his hand and told him to feel where the knife and scissors, or whatever, had cut Quiescan free, smoothing him out and rendering him sexually silent. *What for?* John wondered. *Surely she has not told me the full story. All for the plague?* He asked. She told him Quiescan's enemies had used the plague as an excuse. Who, he asked. "Oh, his old students," she said, whom he had rebuked. "They severed him in the end in the usual tradition of strike the father dead. You will have heard of it. He and I travel together, both being rather bookish. Where we come from, where we hover ruminating, we sit inside a large cape, two in one, and this gives him a sense of belonging. For the most part he lives in a gutted dream, yearning to be again what he cannot. He is ideally qualified for the monkish life, but he refuses it. He is one of the true seers. He is an absence contemplating the rest of Creation. He reeks of pork, he coughs blood, and his skin becomes rougher and rougher, like wheat."

Was Quiescan going to speak, having presumably heard all this? All he did was produce a candle and massage it between his hands, whose enormous heat soon softened it, from which he then fashioned not what

John expected and dreaded but a small wax doll. He no sooner finished than Amaryllis removed the red damask bag from herself and popped the doll into it, handing it to Quiescan, who at once began to harangue the bag in some unknown language, not Latin or Italian, while holding it at arm's length. *Envenobia dolst*, he said. "What did he say?" John was willing to learn it; he wanted to talk Quiescan. "It is the language of the broken," she told him. "It is bits of all languages, but mostly sounds he invents at the moment as expressing his feelings. He is a provisional speaker when he is one at all; when he talks, you witness the tragedy of one who talks for the sake of talking. He is quite sincere. Since nobody can be taken in by what he says, he feels free to say anything, and he does." It was as if Quiescan had had the doll and the bag forever, so fast did he incorporate them into what seemed his daily spoken ritual. He is like Banquo, John decided, come to terrify: a ghost yet not a ghost, a ghost with intentions, pain, and the requisite amount of natural anonymity.

Clearly Quiescan had decided to become more interesting, more complex: not the man of the hour, but someone of weight, except that what he began to do, standing on the smeared wood of the floor, his weight somehow concentrated directly down through his boots, sucked in from the outskirts, was unworthy of his sufferings. Without troubling himself, John had noticed the sowbugs infesting the place. Little black shell-backed ovals that sometimes showed a surprising turn of speed, they undertook long treks across the floor, from wall to wall, now and then taking along an offspring that just about kept up, or the parent slowed down. Quiescan, with a delicacy belying the heaviness of his frame, just touched them with his boot, edging them sideways, both adults and babies. At this the sowbugs rolled up into a defensive ball, possum near the giant's tread. He then crunched them flat and moved on, only inches away, to the next dawdler. Little black smudges dotted the floor, of the dead, but other bits of black began to occupy the corners where Quiescan's boots could not reach, though they felt his thunder and perhaps saw the huge avalanche of his hobnailed sole coming down. Imagine, John thought, some monster as much bigger than ourselves as he is than sowbugs. The huge foot coming down, splashing our tripes and smashing our ribs. One buffet and all we ever were is slop. It happens so fast that we have no knowledge of the event, in the middle of a tender or rebellious thought: the whole thing punched writhing out of us, converted to indiscriminate slime blood-red and brain-white. Presumably Quiescan would wipe out all sowbugs lurking inside the walls and under the floor, if only he kept at it; at his present rate, he would put paid to fifty or so each day, but there would always be more of them than he could kill. Back in the runnels and knotholes they would breed and multiply as if anticipating his onslaught; indeed, God had created them with onslaught in mind from other creatures than Quiescan. They asked little: just some damp and a little contributive muck in which to squirm and jubilate within their limits. Black and craunchy (as John's time said for "crunchy"), they personified the ignominious, the lackluster, except to the dedicated few peering at them through a magnifying glass, looking them in the eye.

Rebuking himself for not knowing their Latin name, John resisted the temptation to invent it, certain he knew too little. Something forlorn and dun troubled him. He caught himself wondering if the Almighty took cognizance of all creatures in their shoals and squadrons and hosts and flocks. Or did God only heed categories? Quiescan was the murderous god in the room at that instant, like the blackening Dog Star, which was at its height when summer's heat scorched all vegetation (one try). He was in tune with those wild Greek fantasias in which Orpheus was torn to bits by drunken followers of Bacchus, and his head floated down the Hebrus to the island of Lesbos (second try, as if he, John, were suffering through some tutorial). Enough had been done to Quiescan that he seemed at home among savage and lurid acts, himself poignantly barbarous, almost willing to live in a tub with a homemade candle: a reed dipped in tallow. He was almost at that point, asking the world about him not to entertain him but to lay him bare, readying him for his first and last incorporation into the universe. After which—Well, why bother wording that? John the adorer of words felt their futility, felt that the Almighty, the source of words, was not a verbal entity, that He took the blame for languages but used none. Was that why Quiescan pounded the sowbugs, held to his sexual repertoire even though the bird had flown, wore his nautical hat? John asked himself if he was living inside an allegory devised to make him wiser, but he abandoned the idea, since none of what was happening today made sense, as Chappell liked to say. If Amaryllis had initiated him, Quiescan had merely puzzled: an itinerant entity born to sadden youths of seventeen who for the first time found a nipple in their man o' war.

"He kills them all," he said.

"Mice as well. Spiders, earwigs, beetles. His boots reek of tiny innards. He is trying to balance things up. You can't blame him for feeling godlike. He is getting his own back."

"For castration."

"For castration."

"I do not know what I'd do," John said. "It is truly dreadful. He pretends."

"Oh, we all pretend," she said. "He happens to be very good at it."

"Visibly."

"He thinks of himself as my *cavaliere servente*, whereas, poor fellow, he is much more my servant."

"Your whipping boy, too."

"And my chastener. He likes to remind me of all the waste in the universe. Or if you prefer small allusions, in backstreets like this one. All that he does reminds me of brown crust on the bottoms of pans."

John thought he saw Quiescan marching through London town as the prince of sweet anaphora, the archangel of spendthrift imitation, his emblem a black cone on an old plate—some ten thousand sowbugs fused together in death, yet capable of being delicately roasted to make for him a haunch of tickly viand. Whatever the fellow was, John would be able to make use of his image in later life. Quiescan came from where all other images came from. He was simply more available, made real for local convenience, come home to roost three-dimensional. It was like, John told himself in his well-tempered way, inspecting the word *"figment"* and discovering it enclosed a Roman lady shaping, a Saxon lady shaping bread, and the walled paradise in which she made her bread. Clearly the paradise was one envisioned by her husband, for whom she toiled while he crusaded. A wall, he mused, made of clay, or of mud bricks; why not a wall made of dough? Once upon a time, kneading bread was much the same as kneading clay. People had little to eat. Much as the people within the word leapt to his eye and his mind, so had Quiescan burgeoned in his life, to instruct him, but most of all to ravish him with illustration. The man was an accidental emblem, bound soon to be crushed like a sowbug unless he found a corner of heaven to hide in.

"Late," he told Amaryllis.

"Timeless," she said. "Do not be taken in by the appurtenances of truth. Everything seems normal, but fractionally it is not. I take longer to blink than any human. I misdigest my food, such as I get. One leg walks faster than the other, but only by a tiny amount. My lungs are lopsided. My breasts, your happy hunting ground, are exactly the same size as each other—enough to prove me nonhuman. Spare me the scrutiny, dear boy. Muses are never peered at. I could give you this very moment the materials you will need to do what you are bound to do when you are fifty, but our way is grudging inch-work. We love you to pay in blood what you are certain to receive. Call it pedantry on our part. We have lives. We are not perfect. We are not crystals or clocks. When we are in love, we give and give, but we leave a few claw marks to keep you all, you poets, from getting above yourselves. We all have that somewhat chubby-cheeked look, and quite a few of us have the look I call Sideways Marmoreal, a kind of neuter aloofness."

Quiescan at this point crunched a cortège of sow-bugs with enough force to smash the head of a snake. "You see?" she said. "This mastodon has no muse to refine his behavior. He is unregenerate man, unfit to be even a slaughterer. I consider him ephemeral, a locum tenens, if—"

"Of course," John said. "But if he is that temporary, who replaces him?"

"You do," she whispered. "Be easy. When he has been sufficiently malformed, he will go and you will come into your own, mainly in English, my dove."

THAT SEEMED TO SET QUIESCAN OFF INTO THE FIRST sustained example of his talking power. Beginning with something almost an underfed shout, he soon dwindled into a malevolent moan, seeming to lose heart, or direction, but clearly provoked. "I *am* a man," he began. "Look at me. What do you see? Only what is left. I have a heart, a mind, a fair sense of geography. I am no little shit, really, though you may think I am nothing to take seriously. I have loved and fathered. So many times I have almost died. Not a limb of mine that has not been broken. Not an organ I have not insulted. I used to stamp on crickets, but that required an agility I no longer have. My, how they jumped as I approached, some actually landing on my boot. I would feint this way, then that, to get them giddy, then slam my foot down as fast as I could. They have long legs like giraffes. Now it is sowbugs, as you know. Slower, less likely to leap. I have served in courts and taverns, on shipboard and in the great universities. The only trouble has been that when you add up all my skills, I do not quite come together. Call me a miscellaneous man. Patchwork, motley, that is me. You have to have patience or I go off. I mean I either leave the scene, making you wonder what you have missed, or I explode. I go up in smoke, see. I have what they call an opportune temper—a bad one, mostly—though I have been a great lover, men, women, boys, horses, without ever quite finding what I truly wanted. All along, I have been qualifying for a test that would never take place. Signora here, she saw that in me and took me under her wing, a dark and fleecy place in which sometimes I have wanted never to come out. She tempts me, though, and out I come, like the Queen of Sheba from a thundercloud. Fetch and carry, she said, that hot day in Taormina, and I will see you regularly fed. Perform certain down-to-earth services, and you will be rewarded. When they gelded me for plaguing, she told them who she was and that she would inflict the whole world with a hundred years of bad music, bad writing, bad painting, but they laughed at her and snipped away. You can tell how seriously she took them. Myself, I think she could have landed them with a much worse badness than she did, but she's a kind muse she is, the only black-skinned one I know, not one of your familiar ones at all. She is as likely to dress you in white and bring you ambrosia as to lose her temper. A proper love, she is, even if her legs do start twitching once in a while. Jactitating, she calls it."

John smiled approvingly, delighted to hear a speck of Latin, even if at one remove, but he barely had time to savor the syllables as Quiescan jabbered on, warming to his chore.

"*Jackying*, we say. *You're jackying again*, I say to her, and she says she's sorry. Then I tell her to wriggle her toes and ankles as much as she can. That often stops it. *Jacky*, I sometimes say, and she thinks I've said jerky, which would be almost as good. When it goes on for too long, I start to talk like a real countryman, see, not one of your London tearabouts, and then she has some trouble following me. Italy she comes from, but it's really Zanzibar. *Har you jacky agine?* I says, getting my aspirates all wrong, but she never answers. So I say it again, with a bit more variety in the style: *Har you jackyin' agine, signora? Shall Hoi rub yer feet fer yer? Ho, yus, I'd better. Me hands is just nibblin' to go, to get to work.* That's how it is oftentimes. She puts up with my blather and I rub her feet as if they were two stillborn puppies. Next thing we hear is a little chelp and she's right as rain. Sometimes her mates come to call, and then we have a high-flown time. Turps and Polly, they show up and get together. Turps is properly Terpsickory and Polly is the one known in the trade as Polly-him-near. Dance and Mime, see. These two, Turps and Polly, they're the scriveners for those two, see, as if they was appointed by royal command. Something like that. They *are* not those things, but they rule the roost when inspiration is being handed out. Sometimes, when I let out with *Turps and Polly here, signora,* she gets cross and tells me to say their names aright. Ho, yus. *Two old bolsters to see you, darling*, I tells her. *Two little arse-bleeds from the old country, moddom.* They go to bed together, and oh the twisting, the lip-smacking, the combinations, what with those two so good at pulling faces and doing the ontrashat, and her the muse of poetry, they really start frothing about. Her other name, she says, was Cal*i*ope, but all that got changed during the plague, and I'd have ended up calling her Cally or Cal. Now, how would you like like Cal? They jump and writhe about, then they start licking one another with funny little cries: words like silk and tender and gumdrop. I look away. That's why they call them muses. They amuse themselves, and then they go their separate ways and get on with the job of inspiring. They sit on their heels, wishing somebody to be good, and somewhere somebody is. That's the theory, anyway. Good pulling faces, good dances, and good poems. Some good poems do not rhyme, so I have been told. Once my name was Gloops. It rhymed with "droops." Understand me, then, young sir, I am the handy man to these ladies. Ho, I ham. I do things wrong, but the ladies forgive. I am like the eunuch in the harem, you see. No harm from me, but a lot of puffing. I have all the charm of a man without any of the snags. They say I am really one of them, and they get me to dance, or they did, and when I do, this quaint little smell comes off me like resin."

"Rosin." John was wondering.

"Resin, young sir. No questions. Questions later under the spreading chestnut tree. No more questions.

Thank you. These are special ladies, a little like buyers. They travel and put their foot down, see. *Oh, that is so ugly*, they yelp, and whoever is running the shop or the bazaar or the studio where they are has to burn it. Or they say, *Oh, so beee-yewtiful*, and then that person gets promoted away to some pavilion where they have to work even harder, seeing that the world needs beautiful things more than it needs the other—well, it is obvious. These women are inspectors. Nothing worse than a case of bad mime, spread over a century, though they tend to catch it before it has gone on that long. Worse than bad mime, though, is bad dancing. That's really a disease, so poor old Turps, she has to tramp out and about, stopping them all from getting too near to one another. All bad dance gets condemned, and the dancers too, though she finds it hard to tell a bad dance from a bad dancer. Signora has it worst, because you have all these delicate young fellows scribbling in haylofts and lighthouses all over the world. She has to get down on her hands and knees and see what they have done, and as often as not she lets out an awful shriek: *There's only so much inspiration*, she howls, *only so much corn for all the chickens*. Really, she wants them all to stop writing, and to anyone who promises not to start she promises a small farm in Burgundy or the Midi, somewhere south. But they scribble away. She is the muse that has to vomit most. She cannot abide the stuff. She is trying to think of better bribes."

"I hope not," John said dejectedly, with his hands clasped then rammed against his mouth. "Not for me. It is poetry, not the clergy, for me."

Quiescan had not even heard him and was moving into more serious terrain, telling John how to propitiate his own muse, not tickling her, not blowing in her ear, not tugging her pubic hair, not biting her nipples. "I'll do anything," John told him, "to get in her good books. I'll even eat—"

"Thousands have," he heard, "and it has not got them far. Kiss her with a closed mouth, boy, and she will respect you for it. Press hard, and breathe evenly. Do not pinch. Do not cough."

Then it came: the truth about the muses, insinuated into Quiescan's account of an orgy when they all got together, all nine of them. He was the offal-eating oaf in the mask leering out from the bushes. The muses were hard on their best performers, he said. They cared little about the hacks, the money-grubbers, whom they mostly allowed to go their own way. No, the mimes, dancers, and poets, and all the rest they were hardest on, were the geniuses and near-geniuses, handing them harsh lives and almost constant humiliation, hunger and scabs, drear loss and chronic insomnia. "The signora, for example," he said with an uncleared voice that did not quite achieve its customary timbre, "will roll about on grass or bed, purring with approval. Next thing, she will say, *Give him the pox to see what it makes of him*. That is how she behaves, young sir, a perverse and putrid bitch at her worst. They go on serving her, though, as if she had sucked them off. It is said that although these muses— women of much fungus, I might say—give themselves to the arts, and all artists, it is Apollo they love. He runs them like whores, and they dote on his cruel ways."

John was caught between worrying about himself and the odd assortment of company he was in. On the one hand, did everyone have millracing thoughts as he did, a mind like a volcano *and* a waterfall? If so, did people find it just as hard to keep pace with all that bustled through, the horde of silverfish that everyone called thought? On the other hand, why should someone as exotic and cultivated as Amaryllis (if indeed she were Calliope) have as her squire someone as dividedly-minded as Quiescan, part oaf, part conscience of the ages? If she could have Polyhymnia and Terpsichore as friends and allies, did she need a buffo eunuch to keep things moving? Convinced he had missed something about his own internal processes (or those of others, which was likelier), as well as about Quiescan, John set to wondering if he should make a bolt for it. Would some malign aide of Amaryllis strike him dead before he had negotiated the first set of stairs? Was that Quiescan's role? To apprehend the escapee and bring him or her back? He was heavy enough to do some damage to a thin, short youth, but surely Amaryllis, if endowed with all manner of ineffable power, could stop him dead if she chose, paralyzing him with badness.

ALL THIS TIME, AMARYLLIS HAD BEEN LISTENING WITH the air of someone chastened, willing to listen but not to take it seriously. "He gets like this," she said, "when we have to go. We shall shortly have to try somewhere else, probably on the Continent. We cannot stay forever, charming as the company is. He frets and talks because, each time we leave, he has in a sense to go down. He becomes disposed of, so to speak, and then he comes back refurbished. At least you and I, John, have had our encounter. There is one thing about being a muse: you avoid the other muses like a plague, except for one or two; otherwise you have to rub shoulders with them, and painters are everlastingly lining you up, or arranging you like cut flowers, to make up a pretty pattern. I would rather be a trollop, but you have to take what is given you, in this life and any other."

"Any other?" John said. "You have others?"

"Don't *you?*" She tossed her mane of black hair and brushed his question away. "I get tired of him. I like to see things neat and folded. He's untidy. I like a nice clean tablecloth and a gleam from the cutlery. He will eat off a piece of board sheep have walked over. I like peace and quiet. He likes hurly-burly."

"He's a page of sorts," John said gently.

"I'm a page *of sorts*," Quiescan told them. "But I'm more than that. I am salt, chicory, poison, gunpowder, sap, damsons, cuckoo eggs, chalk, spurs, and sacking. I inhabit everything. I bring to all transactions what is needed. I bring matters to a boil, sir, and when I go abroad, in the sense of sauntering out, I apply myself to whatever I find. I bring report back."

"Is that how you find poets? If so, are there not easier ways? An advertisement?"

"Not random enough," he said. "We do scour the ancient universities, of course, the taverns, the gaols, the banks of the Thames, but we rarely find anything. Who was that last one, always sucking his tongue as if it were the last sweetmeat on earth? The pink-flesh man who talked about plumped-up pillows and perfumed bed-linen? Spen—?"

"—ser," she snapped.

"If I had my way, son," he murmured, seizing John by the shoulders, "I'd set out with a razor. Kill most of them on sight, I would. So very few of them come to anything. And once they do, she tightens up the screws on them, which just about stops them. They have to be very persistent to get anywhere once she's decided they are good."

"Don't you believe all that old codswallop," she said. "Good taste drives him frantic. Some of them are real finds. Usually lacking in character, but a few quick downfalls or some sustained bonesplitting pain usually works the trick. Then they begin to shine even as the cancer gets its pincers into them and they cough enough blood to fill an inkwell. Once I hear them coughing and whining, gasping and raving, I know they are just about to qualify. We of the old school set great store by suffering. Who wants poems from the untouched? We usually try to make them hurt as much as possible without quite blowing out the flame."

John backed away from her dab hand aimed at his midriff. "I am just starting out. There's no need to worry about me for years."

"We won't," Amaryllis said. "But one of these days we will come for you, and yours, if not with a plague, then with mind-sundering grief. People like to take their poets seriously."

"Oh," John said, as his face froze and refused to obey him, "I will be ninety before I even begin. At least keep the plague at bay till then. Then it can have me. Once I'm started."

Quiescan took up her refrain now, pointing to different parts of his inflated body as their fate came up. "She's a champion with toothache and the way it kills sleep. Headaches so bad that those who have them take an ax to themselves and split their heads asunder. Pain and dastardly acceleration of the heart is a favorite with her. Then the Neapolitan bone ache, the crabs, the gout, the stone, the tapeworm, piles, the ague: she does all that, and with grand style. I tell you, sir, some who hear this give up verses—or paint or melody—and solicit their fates prematurely. The fear is so great they no longer wish to be aware of anything."

"Then, signora," John asked, "instead of being my muse, are you not Death? Surely Death cannot also be Poesy. Where is the sense in that?"

She explained to him with taut gravity that all muses kill, that art, as one way of not going mad, implicates its practitioner in the mechanisms of fatality. To write well, she said, is to invite death to do its worst, to defy all the forces arranged against the mortal soul. To create badly is not to enter the tournament at all, whereas to excel— "That," she said, "takes on the gods at their own game. If you understand me. I mean, dear boy, that you may well end up with an ivory shoulder for composing one superb stanza. Or with an appalling stench coming from your backside even at the best of times. Your teeth may turn to water. Your children may drop dead. You may go blind or deaf. I am sorry to harp on this, but beware of doing well, for upon those who do we push. The Furies will take you by the short hairs and redefine for you the nature of agony."

"She is very good," Quiescan was mumbling, "with the hard phallus that will not go down. Imagine the pain. And the slow turning of an eye to stone, like a glass marble that has been filed."

"Bosh," she said, fumbling with her little red damask bag. "This thing reeks."

"Do not trust her," said Quiescan. "She has been employed thus for far too long and, instead of being the velvet-skinned young Negress you see before you, is an old harridan dead and reborn so many times she can be folded up and slid into a pocket. Without me—"

"Without him," she said, "I would have had mime and dance to myself before now. God's blood, what do I have to do to make myself more useful?"

"Then I will not," John said. "I will stop."

"Already decided, you cute little rhymer."

"It can't be," he said.

"Try it. You'll see," she told him with imperious pique. "Your day will come. The first of them has already started. I can see it now. You are going to be a lot of trouble to your near and dear, and you are going to endure much of it yourself. We have plans for you."

"Tell me, then," John shrieked.

"We want to see if you can resist. In the human order of things, as seen from the catalytic cliffs of the firmament, this is called the test imposed, meaning the award given. You are as a dog on an unbreakable chain. Bark, sir. Nothing will change."

"What a hateful universe."

"Rather," she scolded, "think of it, John, as a very strict grammar school, in which tutors are themselves flogged to make them flog you all the harder. To make you excel. More godlike. If you fail, the flogging will cease. If you shine, we will half-kill you to see how far you can be pushed. What is more Platonic than that?"

Almost ready to weep, John pulled back from such an overt display; muses could lie, and bombast could fade. Or so he assumed until what happened next.

ONCE DEGRADED, ALWAYS DEGRADED, JOHN THOUGHT. Once schooled in a hovel by the demon muse, always in a hovel. I was not looking for her. I was—what is that quaint expression coming from who knows where?—brained by her beauty, by the weird chance that she seemed to take a fancy to me, even to my face, with its lugubrious taper, my overlong nose drooping toward the rosebud mouth like an excommunicated tuber. Almost a girl, like Quiescan, I have big, soulful, but untempting eyes—the eyes of one who knows too much Latin, has pored over too many fusty books. I dangled like a fruit to be plucked, not for poetry, but for sex and excess. Now I have been sliced up like a potato and am soon to be cooked. I am less pert than I was. I am going to pay the devil for being gullible, and I will be sent packing with, in my pocket, a phallus carved from soap, a little red damask bag, and a sure dose of the plague. If this be poesy, make me a blacksmith. Imagine: I have hardly penned a hundred lines, and here I go, singled out for horror, as if this entire experience were taking place on another level, where it becomes a simple equation in profit and loss. Look at them now.

The other two were packing, bundling up some foul-looking blankets into a round wicker hamper, from which, John swore, as the blankets went in, a rat popped out. He had already asked where, but had been rebuffed. Could he go now? No, there was another stage to be gone through, if he would only be patient. Amaryllis walked around the room at a fast totter, cursing whatever got in her way, while Quiescan intoned various formulae that ended in a complex rhyme. Perhaps he too was a poet and his battered state was typical of what happened to poets. Was he then a good poet, as logic would suggest? At least if you believed Amaryllis.

"Now," she whispered, too loud, "he comes into his own."

"No I bloody don't," Quiescan shouted. "You watch her, lording it over everyone."

"Pest!" she snapped, hurling some loose bundle of cloths at him. "Fold these." If ever John had dreamed that electors to the blessed condition of Poetry would be sleek debaters, now he knew better. The honor, as such, came from a knockabout world as vulgar as tavern songs. The muse was an intensely sexual black slut, but a slut all the same: a brash beauty down on her luck and spoiling for fights. How on earth to placate her, if she were real?

Here she went again, augmenting his image of the muse as a termagant, wearying him with her plaint. "The trouble with all those painters," she announced, as if in farewell greeting, "is they never show what we stand for. All very well for her who represents Mime, or Dance, but how can you tell her who is History from her who is Poetry? There is something too interior about us, not that we should have boards on us stating what we do. I just don't want to be taken for somebody else."

"Well, you *are* black, aren't you?" John wished he had kept his mouth shut. "That is a start, isn't it, signora?"

She stared unpoetically at him, then said, "I want to be known for poetry, not pigment. Where I came from, poetry was far from commonplace, but everybody had this color skin. How would I look poetic? To whom?"

"Well," he answered, "I do, don't I? At Cambridge they call me the Lady of Christ's."

"You mean effeminate."

How tell her? Perhaps she was right, but his Cambridge chums equated effeminate with poetic, and that was that. It was time to go, up those stairs and down, toward what uncouth apocalypse he had no idea; he felt drawn to her, greenly, as before. He had no idea what to believe, being, as he estimated, no more gullible than most. Had he now been received into the company of the potentially gifted: those who, despite storm and quake, fire and plague, would eventually figure in the roll call of the world's poets? He was modest enough, but ambitious, too, reasoning that if he had to bear the insults

of the hearty-horsey set at Cambridge for looking somewhat sensitive, he deserved the status the insults implied.
It was only a matter of writing enough, soon enough,
before the hideous retaliations she had mentioned came
to spoil him. Seventeen was early enough to start, he felt,
preferably in Latin, the tongue of educated folk throughout Europe, although restricting him a good deal when he
wanted to write something racy, in tune with the
ephemeral age and its vulgarities. Still, if Amaryllis and
her pander Apollo were on his side, he might find some
help forthcoming. They would tell him when to break
forth in his own language, putting pompous Latin to
flight. He could hardly wait to get home and write the
news to his friends.

His temptation, of course, as he sourly realized, was
to believe in all that had gone on: in his vision or dream,
concluding that, if there was one thing a poet should trust
in, it was his imagination and what it imagined. He had
no idea how to tell a prophetic vision from an idle imagining, but he was sure it had to do with the atmosphere,
the air pressure, the tightness or looseness of his blood.
From now on, he told himself, it would be work, work,
believing in himself at his most reckless, his most suppo-
sitious, as if even the most far-fetched airy vision could be
fleshed into reality by sheer toil. Even if the starting point
were a hoax, it would not matter if, thinking it genuine,
he went on to slave away. *Misprision*, he thought. Why
not say "deliberately misunderstanding" instead? No,
"misprision" sounded more like the crime it surely was.
Well misprision might mislead him into thinking there

was a career, a vocation, when there was nothing at all, and he should have been a scrivener, a moneylender, like his prosperous father, who doted on the arts and learning with the deflected passion of one who had spurned his own Amaryllis when she came. If she ever did. To aspire hugely, he decided, called for a good helping of self-assurance. You had to invent your confidence, that was all.

At Cambridge they had poo-hooed John for what they thought his high-flown notion of the writer's trade; all, from the brothel-hearties to his close friends and Chappell, had told him to get off his high horse. But he had disdained them, knowing at his core that, when you wrote with harmonious sublimity, you were writing not for yourself or others, but for God, and it was God's eye that escorted you through the most taxing coils of explorative metaphor. It was then you felt most alone, not when merely communicating, but when devising an entirely novel effect to bring into view something unheard of. Some thought this sacrilege, some thought it daft; but John knew, from the shiver and the palpitations it induced, that something uncanny was happening in the style, and being able to do this—even to think of it—set him apart from the rabble, offering back to God, as it were, something brand-new comparable with the first man. When he wrote like that, or thought he did, he was (as he put it) universing, so perhaps this was what had attracted Signora Amaryllis to his side, even if only to shake him up and give him a taste of the unceremonious life. Already he felt the vibrations of what he was going to write. The rhythms of sentences as yet unwritten swayed his brain and coaxed his lips. He had been tapped with the wand long before Amaryllis. He simply had to believe in himself until his heart broke. That he would he had no doubt, voluptuously afflicted with the idea that he had been born to be only himself, and not anyone precious to anyone else—not on the personal plane anyway. God had stunted him, say, to make him bear peculiar fruit, to be the specialist in—what was that process? Turning the world into words that made the world more like itself. Unguided and unaided save by the structure of Roman sentences, he would make verse that outshone a mathematician's lattice, almost not human in its tart finality. All else he would sacrifice to the execution of such stuff, eventually considering himself something cold and bony, like God's two-handed engine. Or if not engine, then shuttle or mortician. He would lay out the language in a spirit of impromptu awe.

He no longer talked of this to anyone, knowing he was doomed to enact it alone, at a divine distance from grocers' bills. Unsuccored, unrewarded, unpleased. The language itself would thank him, perhaps, for deploying, arranging, hefting. He could hear it but not write it, not yet; had he been Virgil he *might* have heard it, because, as he reckoned, progenitors and precursors deserved aural tenderness and got it. Nothing less than the mediation of human sound was going to please him, and if that entailed losing the ability to speak to other humans for months at a time—such was the barrage of euphony coming through—that would be acceptable. Mosaic? Tablets? He smiled at his own bravura, knowing how much he longed for something that final, never mind how mineral.

For God, he told himself: cold-blooded.

For God: indifference to health.

For God: a verbal kennel.

Only two years earlier, the college hearties had told him, as if bringing news of thunder in Philistia to a wincing linnet, a certain Jasper Vinall, playing the new game of cricket, had been killed while preventing an opponent from making two swipes with his bat at the same ball. He admired the man's tenacity and knew that he, John Milton, would give his own life in the quest that faced him. If you wrote for God, instead of seconding him as a clergyman, then your death was a bouquet. There was always death in truly creative composition, much as there had been death before the universe began. He saw his age as XVII, not 17, and knew there was something stark and unapproachable about the Roman numerals: letter-like numerals, these, like turrets or castles, denying access, almost uncouthly defying you to pronounce them. *Ksvy,* he said, I am *ksvy. Eksvie-ie.* I will get older, but I will not give in. Jasper Vinall had come from Horsted Keynes, in Sussex, and John liked the sound of that name; it seemed just as inaccessible as XVII, but his favorite English placename, so far, was Itchen Abbass, which suggested a nun with pox. Nightly, when all was dead and vibration had ceased, he would offer himself up to the words, making that paper song of his longer and longer until it had sung the whole horror and beauty of the universe back to its Maker like a retort from pupil to tutor.

"Really going, John," Amaryllis told him, lithe as a panther, aromatic as a keg of scent. "Our Quiescan has gone before, to get things ready. Come."

MILTON FELT AS IF HE WERE BEING LED OFF TO EXECU-
tion, first treated to a display of the halter, hatchet, and
knife, the stakes and baskets, and his inmost soul with-
ered, his manhood shrank back into the body case, and
the red damask bag in his hands, his purloined talisman,
suddenly lost its power. Something was sucking his
insides out into the spring sun. He was outside, scurrying.
He had negotiated the two sets of stairs without noticing.
There were crowds, but they did not hear his scream,
and they knew nothing of his massive destiny in poetry.
Nor did they know Latin. They wanted to see his head
on a pike, like Fisher's, Bishop of Rochester, from almost
a hundred years earlier, blushing a comely red even
after being parboiled, getting fresher and fresher as if a
superior blood direct from God were coursing through
those treasonous veins. It was as if God had decided to

prove that nothing would waste or be consumed unless—
Ah, that was why he remembered it: the Cambridge
theme, rotting like a perpetual elaborate breakfast.
Nothing dies, he told himself, unless God wants it to. Not
even a sterile academic exercise. On, Milton; outrun the
pack; be a lark ambulant.

He who was going to be a poet would see all
others as mere shades on stage, to be subordinated to the
quest for linear perfection. As for the whole idea of sub-
ordinating people to Latin, he loved it; the Romans con-
quered once again, and the poet, emperor of locution,
rode in triumph. He could see his imperious future, hear
the gossips who said, *See what he gave up for this? It was
never worth it.* He saw nothing odd in his being willing
at seventeen to give up so much, as if the vision of respon-
sibility had frightened him already into settling for poetry. Perhaps only a black or Ethiopic muse could have won
him over; he responded to the exotic as to a species of
magic, even while hurrying through the streets behind
Amaryllis, from whose behind a stream of flower petals
trickled down, marking the route for whoever came after,
as if she were bleeding blossoms.

"Come on, lazybones," she kept calling. "The
future won't wait all day." All he saw was that
wonderful long-legged tromp, enough to make the whole
of London follow her, even if eminence in the domain of
poetry awaited none of them. She was a woman of pow-
erful suction, and the nearer she came to the river, the
louder, the faster, singing what sounded like shanties,
which she punctuated with something between a yodel

and a coarse, warbling entreaty. It was all going too slowly for her, since she knew what was going to happen, but Milton wanted to take his time, savoring the onset, the preamble, inhaling the bad bag as he walked, to insure him against the plague, and greeting the stares of uncomprehending Londoners with his best professional smile. On the brink, he was willing to bear the brunt; he asked only to be the boy wonder for the rest of his life: not only chosen but groomed, his head full of verbs that not even the Romans needed much. With these he could torment her, much as he had tormented Chappell, whom he would probably never see again, even if they allowed him back to Cambridge after his rustication.

"Mil—ton!" she cried without turning around. It was the first time she had used his family name. His career was getting more and more serious by the minute, never mind how much he dragged his feet. The drone of plenty filled his ears. He felt glory without even having qualified, although a part of him worried about Quiescan and what had been done to him. Surely the next poet in favor would not have to be a eunuch. God's blood, it was enough to be a recent virgin and an ongoing chaste eclectic.

"Amaryllis!" he called in return. "Wait."

She did nothing of the kind, bustling around corners and along dismal passageways, with the putrid smell of the river coming ever closer. People bumped and shoved him, mainly because he was watching her rather than looking where he was going, and he wondered how many of them already had the plague. Where was Quiescan? If

there already, at some destination, what fiendish prelude
was he getting ready? John, Milton told himself, you have
only to halt, turn aside, and forget glory for ever. Go
home to your books. This whole thing is a hoax. But
some rebel part of him converted faint intuition into certainty, and on he went, lured thus to his death, his ruin,
his disgrace at least. Why had he assumed she was the
mistress of his fate, the tart magician who would inscribe
his name in the rolls of poetry, bypassing all scholars and
fortune-makers? She had come from Virgil. That was it.
What had *he* written? "A sad thing is a wolf in the fold,
rain on ripe corn, wind in the trees, the anger of
Amaryllis." That was what swayed and humbled him, her
anger. He was not ready to offend another tutor, even an
imagined one. Clutching the so-called bad bag, he threw
his head high to catch sight of masts, and of the blue dev-
astation above them where gulls cavorted, cleaving it.
The sky over water, river or sea, had always seemed to
him somehow higher than elsewhere. There was a lofti-
ness, an airy capacitation he had noticed nowhere else,
and it made his heart vault—he knew he was no mere
starer at statues, but a soul ascending, his head a mix of
piety, poetry, and myth. That he was gullible occurred to
him, but the slur vanished as he saw Amaryllis stop,
ascend a short gangplank, and board an anonymous-
looking vessel, part barge, part galleon, looking neither
seaworthy nor clean, but no doubt the court of miracles.
Amaryllis disappeared, and now he broke into a run,
wondering if he would ever come back. Would poetry kill
him? Would she just cackle with laughter and dismiss

him? Or would she set him an examination he was bound to fail because she based it on infamous topics assigned at Cambridge?

The barge she sat in— No. Where had that come from? What other river scene? Surely somewhere in Shakespeare, he thought, cursing memory and desperate to banish the image of Cleopatra, who of course had been quite different and no relative of Amaryllis. If only his head had not begun to buzz the instant he set foot on the vessel, noting again rats that scampered away, an odd white spume that coated what little was in view (boxes, a bundle of furs, some old bones tied together with red velvet cord). Were the poets of old (of *Eld,* he corrected himself) talking to him, wishing him well, reviling his gift? Could it all be Virgil, using his many voices? Was Amaryllis testing him with ventriloquism, what the Greeks called speaking in the belly? Belowdecks, she and Quiescan seemed to be arguing, but the sound came up dispersed and shredded. No one invited him to descend, but down he went, noting the papery quality of the wood, the stench of decomposition that increased the lower he got. Down and down he clambered, amazed that the vessel went so deep. Seeing nobody and, now, hearing neither of them, he began to call in a timid, uninvited voice, then more loudly, in his intonation something of what went into those Greek sentences that presupposed the answer Yes. "Are you there?" He coughed, glad he was not a barker. "Quiescan?" which he said as "Quiscan." Finally he called out for Amaryllis, but she was right behind him, glistening black in the poor light, urging him to follow her into a narrow aisle surrounded on either side by what at first seemed sacks, or pieces of cattle wrapped in muslin. No, they were corpses, ungainly and white and indeed in muslin.

"These are the dead," she said. "Look into their mouths." How? No, the mouths were wide open right behind a hole cut in the muslin wrappers.

"Think," she said, "about how the words you are going to use came forth from the mouths of these dead. Just imagine the first cry of the baby and the much later death rattle, if they were fortunate. Any honor you may have resides in these mouths." He was obliged to kiss them all, she said, inhaling deeply as he did so. This was the trumpet of talk, he thought, afraid to vomit into it. One day, someone will do this to me, though none of these, surely, is a poet. He asked and she told him that the poets, what she called the working sample, were higher up. Was he then to kiss them, too? Far from it, she said: his role was to regard them in silence, and then surpass them. "It is not poets we care about here," she said in her prancing voice, "it is the language of the ordinary person, the way the first words formed in the anatomy of the mouth and throat. You will be writing in the language of the dead. All languages, if they have ever been used, are languages of the dead, and you should tremble whenever, as it were, you play with their toys, fire their weapons, filch their sentences from them. They were here. Now they are still. Quiescan happens to be their custodian. He rinses the mouths and applies to them a preservative lotion from Sardinia. Peer into the mouths and imagine the cascade of words coming out. When you write, imagine your words not only in these mouths but in these heads, churning about, festering, at last being sorted out, clumsily of course, until— Well, imagine it, and humble yourself."

"I will," he answered much too fast.

"No, afterward," she said, "after you have thought."

"I am always thinking," he told her. "So there will never be an after."

"Some," she said, giving him a stern look as if vowing to take him on, young as he was, "will prate of expertly carved sprays of roses, doves and daffodils, lilies, Alexander roses, ivy leaves, hearts and crosses, the white marble of Carrara, sculptured angels, curved rays from the morning sun, so-called Old English script, the Shepherd gathering up His lambs, rebated curbs, chamfered curbs, bands of laurels, angel posts, head blocks and rubbed granite, marble white to blue-white in color, the fine, hard limestone known as nabresina that weathers well, gray-white fossil marble ideal for graveyards that forbid white marble, hard cream limestone that forms a weather face after being exposed to the atmosphere, and, oh, Welsh gray-blue slate, Yorkshire stone. Just about any substance that can be sawn, dressed, masoned, carved, and polished or sanded, and green fossite chippings, plinths on sloping ground—all that—on behalf of death, and it just is not worthwhile. This is better. I especially deplore gravestones carved to resemble an opened book. No, this is better: to have the simple slip-in berth, with all manner of one's fellows arrayed about one like seeds in a flower. I want you to ponder the dignity of the dead, whose idiom you purloin. View them, smell them, caress them. Without the language they created, you would be helpless, creating a mere impromptu mumble that nobody understood. Do you see?"

"Verily," Milton said, trying to be august, ancient, and solemn all in one word, his mind on the simple elementary fact that it was still spring and still the same day. A lifetime had tunneled through him, almost annulling his youth, loading him with destiny and chores.

"Just as well," she snapped. "We muses, tolerant as we are, have certain aversions, such as the inscriptions used to salute the dead with. I even have some of these by heart. 'A tiny flower lent, not given, / To bud on earth and bloom in heaven.' What do you make of that, Milton? Here's another: 'Out of the depth I have cried to thee Lord, / Hear my prayer.' They always omit the comma for the vocative, and their ditties never end with anything so coarse as punctuation. Another one that comes to me is this: 'Father in thy gracious keeping / Leave we now our loved one sleeping.' It is not that we are harsh. We are not, but we believe that standards must be kept up. Hence your charge, young Milton, to compose verses we shall not wince at, granted that the rest of the world may not care and has no taste. You shall write as if people did care, so that those few shall be satisfied. We travel the world not so much in the certainty that we shall prevail, for we never do, but to maintain a needed attitude. We travel in the interests of art, being especially

severe with our best practitioners, content to let mere
scribblers fall back into the mob. If we discern a gleam of
talent, we twist the thumbscrew hard, so beware, young
John: you have a choice between becoming a genius or a
hack. Go read the graveyards if you lack provocation.
Lean backward to the delicate-souled Virgil should you
need a buttress. Be fair, but never forget that you have
been committed, given over, to an art, which has to be the
most important thing in your life. Hearts may break, but
never your decorum."

At this, young John began to age, having visions
he had no right to, no need for. He heard the meek,
exhausted soul entreating death for surcease, peace, a
painless chop. In a dark-brown melody, death answered
back, only a tinge overbearing and cocksure as the soul
began a series of tiny, delicate taps on a spinet, tentative
and trusting, but awed and shaky. Death became even
more reassuring, saying that all had managed it so far,
hanging back, but at the last coaxed over. *Transii*,
humans called it, meaning *Over you go*, as if over a stile
or a fence, and forever after your body clad lay above
your naked corpse, just to show how they belonged
together, twinned. Again John heard the petty tweet of
the soul going over, aching just to be begged of one last
time, even to be flattered, calling up from those who
loved it the best and tenderest moments from an only-
too-intermittent euphoria, while death, in its voluptuous,
wheedling tenor, said to give up all that: the soul was now
past need. Then, pleaded the soul, annihilate me without
my help, which death answered by opening wide its huge,

sardonic legs and striding out over its preferred terrain, like Quiescan di Garbo.

Low over their imploring faces, all these souls in the offing, loomed a shaggy crotch encrusted with dung, a chain of black caverns with gorse fires burning in the distance, all along the rim, in mauve putridity. John quaked, telling himself he would be the first human to whom none of this would apply. No *transii* for him. No need for him to learn Latin from granduncle Death. He heard the soul entreating Death to kill it in an undeathly way, and Death reciting its vagabond melody about how lovely it was, really, to surrender just before the death rattle, with the giant destroyer straddling the latest recruit, exposing the portals of the promised land.

Then it was gone, the vision that consumed itself, never to return (he hoped) until the day it all came true, no longer a vision, but the next event, in which death the poignant, lonely monster mock-pleaded for what it had already seized. John shook, knowing that terror such as this ensured that you grew younger and younger, backing away into perpetual infancy. He heard the death ditty, preposterous and crass:

> Pity me who sometimes
> Almost does not get
> The promised parcel;
> Oh, the agony of almost
> Always having them refuse
> My unfailing hospice.

Had she finished? Peremptory, tyrannical, callous, coarse, unkempt, insensitive, high-handed, boorish, uppish, questionably qualified, and forever dragging malformed hunks of bread from her pockets to keep her going, she had not only offended him, she had made his blood run cold.

He had never suspected, if he was to believe all she said, he was going to have so much to do with the departed. To this woman, if a muse were a woman rather than a busy effigy of vile commands, the language he loved was a headstone. Surely anyone as ragamuffin as she— tugging a bean, a radish, a potato from her pocket or even some aperture of her body—knew nothing of poetry or art; yet no countermuses came to send her packing. If such existed, why did they not intervene? If she were an imposter, should they not swoop down and dump her in the river? He felt alone and defenseless as she motioned to him to go on setting his mouth and ears against the mouths of these dead, inhaling their spent glory, guessing at their corrupted faces. It was a poor beginning, even for an elegist, which Milton was far from sure he was going to become—an epic poet, more probably. She, she told him, had the wherewithal; she had eaten time; she did not live in time, which lived in her. She had already been to all places that were going to exist, and she had by heart each moment of every poet's career, though she was not willing to divulge.

"Knaibor Boit," she said to him abruptly. "That is one place you have never been, and you will never see it, not even by the day of your death. Remember the name, John, make use of it for generations to come. By then you will be a mere shade on stage. Be tender with your technique, be stern with human beings. You are hereby authorized to sell down the river such of your intimates as impede you. We have seen your first verses. You are going to qualify. We have already seen your last work, sir, something in blank verse. We say this only to torment you."

"Blank?" he spluttered. "And who is this royal we? Who composes the we?"

The muses and the dead, she told him. "We are the dead's congeners, John; we take all the force of their moral suasion and convert it into power. Do you remember your Aristotle?" He did, but he preferred Plato; so they were roughing him up already.

"Entelechy, Master Milton? To the run-of-the-mill

Greeks, it meant a sense of destiny, the consummation of your self. To them a process, an end, but to Aristotle, who must have seemed in a hurry, it meant consummated selfhood achieved—the completed state. Well, we divine your entelechy, in the Aristotelian sense, and, frankly, we burn with impatience to see you on the brink of taking so long. It is one of our flaws, this impatience to see our slaves taking so long to get to where we know they are going. Master Keats and Master Eliot have not even started. Not even born. A huge pack will come after you, aware of you, young-fellow-me-lad, but none of your worry. All are ours, except for their so-called free will: the drug they dote on, little knowing their sublimest trouvailles are things we have kicked out with the morning's ashes, with our spittle silvering them. Sometimes our brainwaves affect those who write without knowing we exist—the so-called lost tribe of scribes who write uninvited and unsanctioned, and sometimes get away with it through a special vote of the muses. Enough. Quiescan is waiting for us, a redhot skull on a pewter tray in his hands."

Up they went to the top deck, where indeed Quiescan stood, on his face an apocalyptic leer.

"The dead are great detainers," he finally said. "Never mind. But we do have business afoot." He thumped on the deck three times. The rats began to leave. "See into the skull," he commanded, and Milton screwed up his eyes against the incinerating heat, saw only tiny golden dolphins swimming or flying in a circle, trying to catch up with one another, but in vain. The entire skull was empty but for them, though it seemed to have different levels within its down-tapering interior. Milton had been peering through the eyeholes. Now Quiescan set the tray down on the deck and motioned him toward the bow. They were going to move out, far from set sail, but slide away, he thought, hoping the river would freeze and jam them in.

Looking sideways at her, Milton reminded himself, without too much groveling pomp, that this woman was the foremost of the nine muses: the mother of Orpheus and the bedmate of Apollo. Now she was mothering him, with rough, expedient hand; fostering, then, with that peculiar look, anxiety and stare-you-down zeal combined, tall in the prow, a female athlete beginning to go somewhat to seed, though not in her apple-firm arms, her tautly modeled throat, or her deep, mounded chin. She swelled lower down with lovely upholstery, oiled black satin, off her coming what he could only describe as vapor of burned butter. She was peering ahead at something Milton could not see, perhaps an aurora of greengages and sapphires, and he congratulated himself on his muse, so different from the chubby-cheeked person in a drawing he had seen, in which she had a look of postcoital ruefulness, her eyes downcast, her lips sucked taut against her teeth. Indeed the other she of the exquisite voice, as the Greeks dubbed her, looked rather like a Germanic trollop, with her hair stacked on top of her head and her heavy-lidded eyes beginning to sleep. They were both exquisite-voiced, of course, but he preferred "his" muse as more stable, endowed with a superior degree of reticence, poise, and drive. Compared with Melpomene, the muse of tragedy, she was a paragon of dignity, never like Melpomene canting sideways, one hand supporting her face, whose expression of histrionic sulk did not bear looking at.

Amaryllis had a habit when pronouncing *th* of extending her tongue far out as if declaring the imminence of the sound, which meant she made it with not quite the tip of her tongue, but with the pulpy cushion a little way back, delivering into the air something almost visceral and visibly lewd. The tongue's tip also flicked the underside of her top lip as, indeed, she made a meal of *theta*, inviting any budding poet to touch tongues with her, to taste the copper and balsam in her saliva. To him she would always be an Amaryllis, not because he doted on shepherdesses, Virgil-fashion, but because he adored the lunges of his impetuous imagination, relishing its spoor and its chatty magnetism. Whatever it called things in the world, that was pleasant to him, and hang accuracy. You never forgot your muse was a muse, but you might overlook, eventually, the salt passion in her nature: Signora Amaryllis as distinct from her royal highness the muse, less a woman than an anthology of preposterous unions, slavering upon the harvest as if it were a map of Poesy.

The barge moved slowly, with an eerie scuffing sound, gaining the center of the river but barely making headway against the tide. Would learned annotators in centuries to come be able to calculate that the tide was against them on this particular afternoon?

Milton wondered at their lack of progress, then recognized they had no propulsive power. His muse was propelling the vessel by sheer will, or the dead below were doing a stealthy battuta with new-picked-up oars. Where then? And why? With him between them, the other two jumped, less a jump than a silky flowering forward, into filthy water, needing not to swim but forging delicately forward as if the prow had fallen off and come to life, mute wooden shoulders and legs coming to timely busyness: an emblem of inspiration willing the barge after it. Amaryllis snorted, Milton gasped, and Quiescan puffed water away from his mouth. They were doing rather well, at least until the barge behind them melted upward in a golden flash, starting at river level and soaring, soaring, with no sign of the corpses now being consumed. The barge had gone, translated into fire, at her command of course, and Milton wondered about the mouths, the faces, the bodies, ravaged with compassion for those who felt no pain.

Now the language was all they left behind them. It seemed like a demonstration, for his benefit; there was more to it than that, but what? Milton was not accustomed to pondering while swimming. Or was it swimming? He ceased to move. He floated now, still pressing forward against the tide with supple persistence, the other two not actually touching him. He was flying, like a flying fish. The water grew warmer, to receive towels or a fish to be poached. Now they were cruising at a steady clip as if the incoming tide were metaphysical, an affair of logbooks, a merely nominal impetus. Nothing barred their way save some drifting logs that miraculously went around them, blasted into cooperation by her seething need to push on eastward.

Floating that way in postures ranging from elegant akimbo to dead man's float, Milton looked downriver for a glimpse of their destination: some shimmering galleon, a temple collapsed into the river, a horned monster agape for their flesh. Then he peered behind, but the shawl of flame had sunk beneath the water; not even a plank or a wooden rib floated back there. He had seen dawn do this, with its pale-blue drained acid burning a hole in the gray around it, and suddenly all was a conflagration of salmon.

He grieved, he toured along on the surface, almost a water beetle, and the other two said nothing, perhaps habituated to this routine, having no doubt swum or wafted downriver with Chaucer, Langland, Spenser, Shakespeare, Jonson. Was he really joining that august, contentious company, picked out in his seventeenth year as, what, a *cadet* poet? Was he that good already, or had there simply been no one else? If other poets came to nothing, how would anyone ever know their names? If nobody ever said their names, how would they ever amount to anything? So was selection this arbitrary, a thing to be over and done with like the rinsing of dishes? It pained him to be—he invented a word for it—aquaplaning thus, made one of the elect through sheer impatience, the standard emotion of Quiescan, Apollo's punching bag. Cambridge would never have allowed such a bald and hurried procedure. Even a Bachelor of Arts degree took four years. So how might a mere youth new to shaving his face become the heir designate in poetry?

The answer was that superb and holy powers were matchless prognosticators, and what might strike onlookers or eavesdroppers as paltry farce or petulant circus was really a hint as to the nature of divine get-up-and-go. Uncouth as the process was, compared with a contest at the spinet, it was cryptically volcanic, akin to pushing someone into the river for the fun of it, or for no fun at all—it was what the muscles felt inclined to do, what they did next. Whether or not, over the next few years or so, he could accustom himself to such whirlpools of opportunity, he did not know; his stomach ached, his eyes stung from aged filth in the riverwater, and a moss-green scum had formed over his lower face, making him into a floating kennel for breeze flies, the frail tap of whose legs drove him into a mighty unpoetic frenzy. One day he would emend the text of his beloved Euripides and earn the scholars' praise for doing so.

A HOUSE WAS FLOATING TOWARD HIM, NO DOUBT loosened from the river's bank by sheer erosion; not a large house, but an elegant narrow one, some half a mile away, nodding on the tide and wobbling although always returning to an even sit. Would a house without a keel float as trimly as that? Perhaps it was not an empty house, either, but something permanent that usually docked and might be lived in. The lap of the water was soothing; the racket of the streets would be far away; the slight rocking of the house might be conducive to sleep, inspiration, and venery. On the whole, he thought, he would like to live in a floating house, rats or no.

But the apparition seemed to come no nearer and certainly did not increase in size. He peered, shouted, took in a mouthful of riverwater tasting of tar and mud. Then the house was upon them, gliding by, then circling

121

against the current as Amaryllis raised her hand and inscrutably commanded it alongside. It was a gondola, freshly painted and sumptuously decked out with velvet cushions and lurid tapestries: not a house but a houselet big enough for two. He was never sure how he got aboard, but the water seemed to rise all of a sudden, buoying him up high enough to roll sideways in, landing on soft bolsters arranged along the side. Amaryllis was toweling his naked body, she naked too, chortling at his thinness while Quiescan poled on against the current, every now and then letting out an uncouth shout in an unknown tongue. It might have been the depth, but if so how did he know it? His pole was unmarked and they were surely in deeper water than he could measure with his rhythmic thrusts. Now John dried Amaryllis, who looked preposterously younger, as if some veneer had washed away in the Thames and she appeared little older than he, a radiant black damsel to his bleached-looking swain. Her small regular teeth flashed. Her lips seemed much larger and almost too thick to be maneuvered in speech; the center of her top lip had somehow bent back to provide a kissing pad. All together she had a juvenile air, stripped of the brash obtuseness he had begun to weary of, and she seemed plaintive now and compliant, his to adore without more ado.

"My, you look delicious," he said light-headedly.

"The proof of the pudding," she told him, not that he needed urging. Now it was as it should have been in the beginning, he thought, as she seduced him with only a tender barcarole missing. Even as Quiescan sang in his bloated baritone, they made impetuous love among the cushions, reaching out at each other blindly and exclaiming with delight. It was a tryst, with no spectator, under a dark-green canopy that shaded them from the spring sun. Anyone looking that way would have seen a gondola sliding out into the estuary, the lonely gondolier a hulk of intent automatism, scything the flood rather than dipping into it, eager to reach his destination. Murmuring with innocent fatigue, the muse and her swain fed on each other, she coaxing him beyond the point at which he knew, he just knew, he would have to cease, and sleep for a week. "You underprize yourself, John," she sighed, "in all matters except poetry. Now, show me again. We are going to be close for the rest of our lives." He tried and was rewarded, closing his eyes against the black sheen of her skin only to find himself in another darkness in which motes swam and feinted against the red screen of his blood. Again he felt the same misgiving: it was all too lovely, too gentle. The haughty, censorious, rough-hewn woman of only hours ago had mollified herself to a shocking extent, visibly the same, more or less, but no more the chiding mother, the scolding aunt, the mordant harridan, the caustic survivor. She was a sweetpuss now, adapted to his every need and making other needs grow in him without warning. Her eyes had lost their unimpressionable glaze. Her hands made different gestures, no longer hacking the air but trailing through it in voluptuous eddies. Perhaps she had other roles, but of the two he knew, he preferred this, having always known—on the basis of no evidence at all—that muses were tenderly feminine rather than infernal machines that just selected and appointed, all in a loud voice while looking the other way. He was willing to believe that she had tested him, found him unintimidated, and had now relented, willing to glide along with him forever while Quiescan the inglorious continued his indefatigable single sweep from the starboard quarter. The prow's beak bobbed and swayed along the distant horizon, bisecting or agitatedly tracing it. *Going out to sea in a gondola*, he thought, unable to identify the echo. I will never return. It will not be the career of John Milton poet, but the disappearance of John Milton infatuated swain, last seen aiming at France with a dark-skinned woman in a gondola. No doubt drowned with all hands. He would return when he was fifty, say, telling them about the joys of monogamy.

He almost lisps, she thought, he is so pleased. He has energy and tenderness. He is no longer in awe of me, or worried about catching some disease. He no longer even believes in the plague. Bless him, then. He will be working hard for the remainder of his life, and not upon a woman's body. I have blooded him and he will ever after wonder what I was, what gender, what species, what shape. My ghost will enrapture him at the most opportune times, priming in him the guilt he will feel for having imposed upon me a name not mine. I will become an eidolon. He will cry for me in years to come, without the faintest hope of a reprise, yet knowing his soul was gentled at my hands. I brought him up as I swayed him back and down, pivoting at the waist as he gasped at the anatomical splendor of it. He will boast, as men do, but no one will believe him, not even the cocksure hearties he calls Cambridge brothelkeepers. They will look and say atrocious things. One look at him, and you know he could have done none of it, which is why, when this spell unwinds, he will find around the shaft of his organ a thick ring of hair immovable and final, like a punitive outcrop. Imagine the trouble that will brew for him. A cunt quoit. I am not often up to such games, having a higher calling I deny only through hotheaded truancy. Why should I not enjoy the search?

I have to rest, however, before the early nineteenth century comes thundering up. There are some hard cases in store, but we will have to take them on anyway. It is pleasant to have been warmed. I will no longer need to brush up on my Latin and Greek. Quiescan will have moderated his ways by then and become almost inured to metamorphoses. And now here comes our John again, with a horn to plunge; he cares not if I be sister, mother, or slut.

Again they joined, babbling and cooing, hugging and protesting, running out of breath and bursting into amorous laughter from the preposterous joy of it all. In back of them, Quiescan toiled aloofly, knowing his duties but wishing himself far away, in Constantinople or Rome, absent from duty, and willing to risk the plague if only he could lead a less haltered, leashed life. Milton was reciting some Latin verses he had penned only days ago, but she seemed little surprised and countered with what he recognized as bits of Virgil. Wine they found, and some fresh bread, so they had a marine picnic on the cushions under the awning as they rounded Cliffe Marshes.

"Don't leave me," John said in a fit of prophetic anguish.

"How can you be so sure I have joined you?"

It was obvious, he told her.

"Just you remember *me*," she ordered. "The best things never last forever."

"Promise," he whispered.

"You can't talk to a muse like that."

"How, then? In Latin?" She kissed him with stupendous pressure, smothering his little mouth. *Osculo osculum suffocavit.*

Now HE UNDERSTOOD WHAT HE HAD HEARD AND
dismissed about the permanence of love; things that
happened in a moment endured for a lifetime; some
things that happened in a flash were *worth* a lifetime.
And some lifetimes did not have a single moment of such
expansive, thorough ecstasy. All this he had heard at
second hand, or read about in Virgil and Ovid and
Spenser: the rhetoric of the heart. Fondling Amaryllis's
back at her request, he felt something selfless and unlust-
ful beginning to stir in him, more a tribute to the Creator
than it was fleshly reciprocation. He wondered how
many of the routine caresses held within them this aloof,
unquesting quality, as if this were the first back, say, and
her breasts the first of those, at both of which—back and
breasts—he looked like a rabbit peering at the first root
of celery, a crow espying the first frog. Something inhu-

man quaked in him, telling him that whatever he might be doing, whether being seduced or performing in his greenhorn way the postcoital honors she seemed to require, he was dabbling with the Almighty's toys: not Milton's, not ever his save by proxy. And this unnerved him, at first, then began to stoke in him a tentative self-esteem based on something like hero worship. God had given them both these parts to play with, and the right response to them seemed less a lewd Ben Jonson-type joke than a prayer of thanks. He hated to become so solemn about passion, but it was his young habit to discern the author of all being in all phenomena. The pleasures of embrace and union, as he mentally put it, paled beside the originality of genesis. It was simply that no poet could match it. He shuddered at the power of the brain whose prolixity sent new things spewing into the void: to think them was to generate them in uncountable numbers, or almost such.

Ergo, as he liked to say, musing that Ergo should have been the name of a nagging, pedantic poet, all poets were derivative. There was nothing ex nihilo in what they did, so it was improper to chide poets for being far-fetched inasmuch as all they wrote depended on something already in existence. This was what came of trying to cope with Chappell's arcane problems in logic and theology. Scratching Amaryllis's back, fondling her feet, licking her ears, palming her curved belly, he almost managed to forget abstruse matters, mainly because he was given to tenderness, but also because he badly needed distraction—as if riding in a gondola toward the open sea with a gleaming black angel were not enough.

She had taken his head in her long-fingered hands and stroked it to sleep. She had honed his private parts to a whole series of performances. She had done countless new and provoking things to him without in the least seeming to need to do so; she did them out of logic, perhaps, since they were available to do. In other words, she was exemplifying herself, evincing the deity—but which deity? Greek or Christian? John had no idea, vaguely supposing that if they attempted something too satanic, a lightning bolt would strike the gondola and send it to the bottom. She was so much more magistral than he, but surely she too, one day, had been a beginner, lying back like an arrow in the full-drawn bow waiting to be fired. He thought of all she could do that she had not done: screaming, insulting, despising, bullying, blaming. None of this had marred her sumptuous tutorship in the gondola, where the laying-on of hands had become a sacrament of almost barbaric gentleness.

He sighed, wishing to sleep, unable to wait for that big suck of gravity as he lay on his side and felt his innards heave into position as if inadequately anchored, then settle leftward and downward, sedating him with weight. Then she tickled him and teased him back to life: not just once, but five times, he thought. The body recuperated endlessly, unbidden, merely fulfilling its nature. He saw now that nothing fell away. Everything remained with you, every lover or enchantress, since all of them were God's. The present one did not efface her predecessor any more than the swan did the gull, or the pigeon the albatross. The many, if that, remained in the reredos of memory, perfectly balanced against a lifetime's desire. There was no priority, as with gods and angels; there was only the successive plenty, the spreading forth of one's habitable body in this direction or that. Without quite realizing it, he had discovered the tang of promiscuity, deeming it godlike, or god-given, and he would have been hard put there in the gondola to find anything against it, much as he was unable to oust Ovid with Virgil or Virgil with Milton.

Nestled in her swarthy arm, he sensed the omnipresence of flesh, its sameness throughout the universe, as if God had made His mind up and left it at that, always creating enough to keep the planet vital but not insisting on too many variations. Always, John would labor to match the world of words with that of the body, wondering what the corporeal equivalent of words was, and always missing it: toe too big, say, pore too small. What were the words of the body, pray? What ratio was appropriate? Shakespeare's Falstaff had once likened politics to the body, taking as far as he could the notion of the body politic, and linking social classes to unminded organs. Easy for Falstaff, he thought. Here was young Milton with his horn in a gondola with a black magician and her rough-hewn henchman. Weary of love, he tried for elegant compliment, but soon faltered for lack of interest on her part. She seemed to have heard it all before, from other poets, who presumably by now had written and moved on. Eyes like olives and breasts like newborn white rabbits fell flat with her and fared no better when he launched into amorous Latin, to which she responded in fluent Italian, which he understood, telling him to quit being so fancy. No guidance, he complained inwardly; no promises, no guarantees, no suggestion of where to go and whom to consult.

A cool breeze flicked against their naked, prone bodies, but neither of them moved, as if there was still some of the spell left and the delight had not burned away a little at a time with each successive cry. "I die," he called out to the sea, and she answered him as if she were it: "We drown, John. We die together." Made nervous each time, he closed his eyes, abolishing the slumping and swilling water, hoping to bed down with her soon on dry land with a cover over them and the door firmly locked.

THE TIDE WAS CHANGING NOW, AND QUIESCAN'S LABOR with the pole became easier, although his unremitting strokes were now so automatic that tide made little difference. He did not notice, not that he had been gondolier that many times. In Amaryllis's service he had learned to obey, to close his mind and eat time. He did what she wanted until she told him to stop. And now she told him. The gondola slowed, twitched sideways, then took up a new tack toward the shore, tussled this way and that, weaving a wiggly course as the tide flowed to a halt and then reversed. It was all in Amaryllis's mind, she told herself; all that happened was in her mind, the flagrant scenery of self-indulgence versus drab reports from those with no power over events. Only Milton had no idea of what was afoot; he had an odd, lancing pain in his eyes, and his groin felt petrified. Sensing only vaguely the gondola's motion, he grew even more passive, yearning to sleep and to postpone all decisions to the morrow. Oh, to get back to Cambridge intact and dine out at the bordellos on his day with Amaryllis.

Before that, however, there had to be a return journey, which somehow he had divined would not be by gondola. Perhaps they would trudge back on foot, cursing the still-dark nights of spring. More than anything he wanted to show her off in college, rapidly losing his reputation as ladylike and demure, strutting into the courtyard instead with this buxom black wench on his arm and potent experience daubed all over his face, his palm cupping a piece of her rear, his shoulder edging the flank of her bosom.

Then they would begin, groveling for a slice from his roast, talking money and favors, even offering their own doxies for a night. But he would calm them with the infatuated glee of a pastmaster, telling them that only very special people, the elect, might traffic with this lady, whose favors were hot-ember blistering, at least to those unaccustomed, and her wrath nothing short of lethal. Like a panther on a chain, she would round on you and disembowel you in a trice, just for licking her the wrong way, south-north instead of north-south. Chappell she would turn to a pillar of salt in a glance, and young men fawning on her at the gate and on the lawns into golden spaniels, born to yap.

"One of your best dreams?" she said.

"Just about my only one," he told her, gesturing

around him. "It's dark by candlelight. Have you ever slept aboard a gondola?"

"You mean: Have I ever spent the night?" Her question struck him as swift and peremptory, as if she were tired of him even if she were growing on him. She was shivering, back now in her buffalo robe. It was time for something hot to drink, but her magic did not include any such thing, she said. Milton wrapped the thickest blanket about him and offered her the two others, but still she shivered, having come from a warmer climate. The gulls following them made a raucous, desperate sound, and fresher breeze cut through the blankets, the buffalo robe. Only Quiescans did not seem to feel the later afternoon cold. Or was it early evening? The sky kept waning and waxing, from a mottle to a mildewed clarity, as if it were no time of day at all, after perhaps an afternoon of unusual heat. Now Milton started kecking, as he called it, from some plague in his middle entrail, heaving over the side, held back by Amaryllis, who was not prey to such maladies. He had eaten little all day, so perhaps it was seasickness and agitation combined. He was no more accustomed to voyaging down estuaries than he was to trifling with muses. The gondola's motion was contrary and uncertain now, each shoreward push the start of an unaccomplished swirl. They could see nothing, these two, but Quiescan had the narrow strand in sight and the marshes beyond, with not a welcome brazier burning, not a light burning yellow in some unnumbered cottage, no crowd cheering their exploit. It was a dismal edge of land, but they all three were glad of it, to them gold dust sprinkled on fresh pastry. In they toured, circling and making the motion of a metronome finger, Amaryllis rubbing John's legs hard to move the circulation, then he rubbing hers and marveling at the primed muscles in her calves, allowing his hand to saunter higher and higher and brush the whiskered vestibule of his afternoon's pleasure. Sighing with pleasure, she doodled idly with his parts, giving him so much verve that they conjoined again even as the gondola drifted to shore and grated to a bump. They took little notice, and Quiescan obediently waited for them to finish. What a wind-swept climax, sharpened with the sense of impending goodbyes!

Unless, John thought even as he felt himself slacken and lapse into a precipitous sadness, they were to be together for months yet as she groomed him for ascendancy, beyond the likes of Marston, Middleton, Massinger, Ford, Herbert of Cherbury, Wither, and the rest, all of them Oxford men and therefore beyond the pale. Indeed, there did seem just now to be a hiatus in poetry, which John had begun to aspire to fill, with or without the sleek supernaturalism of Amaryllis; all he had to do was put the play-acting of Cambridge behind him— false beards, old cloaks, nightwalking cudgelers, salt lotions, and urinals emptying—and he would soar beyond all bawds, buffoons, and mincing Trinculos. He would be his own Quiescan, the mellow galley slave alert at his oar, who addressing the pair of them from behind announced, "We have landed, we are aground, ho, yes."

Each waited for the other to budge, but neither did,

enervated and clinging in the dormant gloom, two cold neuters awaiting stone hotwater bottles for their feet, shawls and muffs, mittens and brass bedwarmers filled with redhot embers, slid between the sheets on long handles. It was not to be. The kissing began again, even as Milton felt the marrow begin to roll down his bones from hip to toe, and Amaryllis knew again the stabbing infarct she had felt every time she sponsored and then released an eligible. "You do it!" she cried to Quiescan, who promptly turned his back and looked away to London, wherever darkness had hidden it.

"Not I," she cried.

"Not what?" Milton said, quaking in his shiver. "Can we go somewhere and get warm? Then we can talk it over, whatever it is."

"You don't understand," she told him. "I have to explain everything. Poets are supposed to be masters of intuition, each a prophet to himself. Blood of my fathers, I want it to be over. In one day I shuttle from forty-five to twenty-nine, and nobody hardly notices. Declensions such as that do not come easily, not even for the likes of you. Now I go the other way and see you watch."

"See you die," he answered without quite knowing what to say next.

"I you, rather than you me." She peered past him into the murk of a London April night and muttered something that both shook and entranced him. "Last year," she began, "there were three losses: Tourneur, Webster, and Fletcher. How am I going to keep a tradition together if they go on kicking the bucket like that? And Middleton has only a year to go. It hardly merits thinking about."

Three dramatists, Milton was thinking. Why all this fuss about *dramatists*? Give me the dramatic poem any day. After all, even if she is a muse, does she oversee playwrights, too? *Tourneur*, she had said, giving the name its full French intonation, instead of "Turner." Why was she so possessive? Could she be the omnivorous muse, generally distributing herself? A busybody? She thinks about death all the time. To her, the plague, so-called, is a mere metaphor for mortality of all kinds. Death itself is a plague, afflicting poets as much as gondoliers. She will be traveling the world looking for replacements. She seems to have an Italian bias, so we know what to expect from them, the Italians. Clearly, though, she can only operate with what she finds; she cannot waft the afflatus into anyone at will. There is still a random distribution of talent, God be thanked.

"I do not seem to have lost my capacity, John, for throwing you into the deep pensives. It is as if the pensive were a case of the noun, somewhere between accusative and genitive!" She purred at her professional quip, then hugged him close. "Light a fire on the beach, *caro*. We have the makings in the gondola." Was she speaking of a *raptus*, that fever of inspiration he dreamed of?

"Hurry, we have not long." She choked.

"Long for what?"

"Call it"—she sighed—"strategy, Milton. You cannot go blundering off into Poetry like a fox into a field. Scheme for it, *caro*. Never go off half-cocked. Tell your-

self that, young as you are, you can have even now experiences well ahead of your years which, one day, you will
squeeze into mature measures. Nothing is ever wasted."

He heard most of this in a boyish daze, hating as
always the tone that warned of impending severance: the
jocular stoicism, the bland imperatives, the inflated
prophecies, the fondly mutational endearments, too
many at one time to carry much weight. When parting,
Milton thought, keep your mouth shut, and then your
eyes. Go numb, and then go. No touch of hand, no kiss.
Here she was, abstractly blustering, as if pain were reme-
diable. "I know what will happen next," he said. "Mild
marjoram will enfold me. Nay, envelop." He took in,
himself steaming with worry and pressure, Amaryllis's
bright words and her fictitious face. Or her bright face
and her fictitious words. He dithered so much that language began to come adrift from events. Doubtless she
had ready for him the veil adorned with saffron acanthus
borders. It was an old tradition, this, abandoning somebody on the beach, or setting him adrift in some flimsy
vessel, gondola or not. It was what his Cambridge friends
jeered at as Viennese: real people marooned in a setting of
purest fakery; thick Armenian paper painted gaudily.
Where was the chair in which he was supposed to sit and
watch them go? Or where were their chairs? Were they
going to drown him after all? How empty the humid air
felt, how warm and clammy the early spring chill. A snake
moved through him, chopping and snipping, and now he
was responding with emotions he had never felt before,
mostly the big shudder that said he was not where he

belonged and the sounds he heard were not the sounds of this place. A cold bolus sat in the pit of his stomach, making him heave. All too soon, he said. What is destroying me has not even had a chance to happen fully. Surely grief has a right to grow, should not have its head ripped off as an overture. More than anything he wanted to be back in that hovel of a room draped with wet skins: by comparison with this place, a place of safety, a nursery, a bower of bliss. He yearned for the stink of tannin and blood, the commotion of Quiescan's abortive tupping, the frivolously convulsive touch of her hand, the one she laughingly told him she kept for "clean duties." It might have been in the Americas, yet it had happened only today, a thousand icebergs earlier, each one a blemished island where love and poetry might not thrive.

Here she came for the final kiss, the unimaginable last hug. He was supposed to feed himself emotionally for the rest of his days. Her face was cold and salty. Her hands felt maltreated. Her bosom shook. She hooted right into his ear. He bawled into hers, knowing now that mother, lover, and whore can merge and become a lasting omission, with the pangs and prods peculiar to each all mixed up and thwarted. She almost fainted, as if she were the one being left, and he reeled on the slopping sand, madly thinking he would dig a channel, a pit, in which to hide with her even as she aged again, her work with him done. "Bite me," she cried. He did. She nearly took his lip off. They rubbed eyes together. He grabbed her hair and made a tent of it, making himself vanish, but it was no use. Quiescan peeled the hair away from his head, even the thick strand between his teeth, and like a bitterly forbearing parent, urged her to be away, to leave what she could not mend. "Ay, a trick become an addiction," she said unsteadily.

"Whatever, signora. End it."

She shoved John off her, but dolphins were coming to rescue him, whom Bacchus had made out of pirates. Unless, like Ovid, who lived near the Tarpeian rock from which criminals were hurled, he was going to be exiled, forever lonely, in sight of London on a clear day.

"Off now," she said, blubbering.

"Oh, no," he shouted. "Not yet."

"Banished," said Quiescan, maneuvering the gondola.

"Tomorrow," Milton said, choking dry.

He felt as if his mind was being rearranged, with magical nudges, his consent unsought. It was almost like—except filmier, less jussive—the first time his penis had limped into stiffness, as if it had gone wrong and he would never again make water through it. Certainly this new sensation was a cousin to that old one. Now he sensed something sleek and silvery being trawled through his brain, a soaring slither with at the end of it a rainbow that made his head pound, as if he had looked at the sun too long. Back then it had been a burlier feeling, making him headstrong and eager to frig the new arrival until a faint, smeary milk appeared on its top, actually seeming to smoke and froth as he whipped it, although he knew such a thing could not be. He had felt, then, somehow defiled and undermined, obliged to minister to his erratic appendage until it ceased to bother him and shrank into its den. He knew his brain, and his future too, had changed from the slime that underhangs a dead fish's belly to something like mercury, bald and heliotropical.

THIS WAS GROWING UP, THEN. THIS WAS GROWING UP in a single day. This was tipping a toe over the edge and tempting the flood or furnace below to rise toward him. The old gods grumbled, flashed their bicepses, coughed up manly brown phlegm from their inmost recesses, aired their penises with grandiose casualness. It was no use; the new gods were in the offing, prancing about and slamming one another on the back, kneeing one another in the loins from behind, making floaty gestures to the rising sun even as their predecessors, homeless and inert, squatted on the grass and broke wind, pottered about with their thumbs, and forbade the coppery-salmon sun to rise on a scene so desolate as this. No use: with the awful energy invested in it from the first, the universe lurched into action, sucking the heart of at least one elect to a dizzy altitude. Milton had risen, out of the slops and the brambles, babbling delicacies and dreaming of a little plague bag, an amulet, he would need no longer, dunked as it had been in death and menses.

Perhaps he was beginning to understand, not as at Cambridge where understanding was by rote at the command of tutors with minds already made up, but through an act of thunderstruck divination. His blood surged and he *knew*, just like that. Surely Amaryllis and Quiescan took the plague with them wherever they went, but where had it begun? He longed to see Ethiopia, but immune. As for Quiescan, mountebank and servant in one, was he not Apollo himself, here to supervise in a bad temper, engaged as often in the mundane enterprises of life? Even poetry had to begin somewhere, even life. How refreshing it was to reason thus at large, in London, no more the pawn of a Chappell, and never mind how preposterous the situation he had landed in. He knew that "preposterous" meant reversed, or back-to-front, and he congratulated himself on knowing exactly the right word. It gave him a sense of power. He was a wizard. He spewed felicity. He commanded attention. He blazed golden. He was Amaryllis's own bard. Only *he* was with them. He saw no other poet in the vicinity. He had come home to land on his feet, however he scanned them.

Now he knew why the birth of Apollo had always so occupied his mind, as an event chaste and, rather than squelching or elastic, silvery and restrained. Again he saw Leto, urgently seeking somewhere to give birth, finally settling for Delos, less a barren island than a meandering rock. Once she had made up her mind, Zeus fastened the island to the sea bottom, and all went ahead: not a distension of thick, fleecy lips with panting and screams. That was too human for Leto, who produced Apollo as a metallic tune, beginning with a tender, fraught appeal, insecurely lilting, then mustered a robust, soaring anthem, thrilled to be yielding up a god that even gods would fear. No one save Leto and Zeus, his father, could abide to be near him, not that he stank or had abrasive ways; he shone too purely, was really a Turk or an Ethiopian, beardless and bronzed. He had, Milton recalled, this dry, plosive quality. Nothing effusive. Or sentimental. Apollo had a lyrical soul all right, but he did not flaunt it, sometimes drab as a husk in sandals, at other times generous without ovation. True, there were times when he throbbed at the sheer deliciousness of being a god and alive and able to control people from enormous distances, but he was always taut, strict, and well tempered. He began his life, Milton remembered, as an armored emanation, not coming out of his mother but rising horizontally beside her, a parallel prodigal. No aura, no hum, no aroma: just a lean, ingenious, and very special shepherd, twanging his lyre even during parturition.

What a subject, Milton thought. Was he equal to it? How would he do a stately largo in words, that astounding first reach toward the world even as Apollo assumed vertical position, like a flame docking? Milton would never have known these things before, but Amaryllis had matriculated him in a day, acquainting him with a god's tangencies and vergings. The strain of being Apollo, which turned pang into unquenchable pain, came into Milton's ears as a sob so prolonged it sounded more like an imprecation. Apollo, he saw now, would always have far too much to do, never have time to be properly dressed, forever have to watch out for wolves and dragons. His special agony, Milton thought: Apollo wanted to be a dolphin all the time, with female dolphins rather than middle-aged oracles or flighty young Daphnes, raving Cassandras.

Capture, then, young Milton told himself steadily, his itch to be other, to go as far away as possible, far past what the aided eye could see: to the stars, back to Turkey or Ethiopia, rather wishing he had never been born at all. Tingling, twitching, seething, fuming, he wanted to be a piece of cooled lava, as untroubled as pumice. Be that god in order to depict him. Yet depict him in what? Best put him into Greek. Apollo's noise was that of noble keening, a well-bred, bruised hauteur coming out, in the elegant baritone of the consummate actor, as plaintive civility. Something cool about Apollo drew Milton on, made him both envious and jubilant, having without homework plumbed the core of him who, naked, kissed the muses and cupped their burly contours in his redhot hand.

As for Amaryllis, tortured by a dream, she ached to know truth unknowable: where she came from, and why, obliged to live in constant disdain for the story Quiescan had babbled once in his cups—a ricochet of a fake cover story told him by God or Jove-knew-whom. It was not worth telling, he said. Did she seriously believe in muses? Did she think this entire escapade was a human thing?

Then what, she asked him. She would never get it, he said, if she did not believe in it beforehand. This seeding of the human race was an old project, continued even though it led nowhere. Almost all of the work written was below standard, but you had to go on hoping. It had never been enough, he said, to find humans interesting and clever: there had to be something else, such as tender self-communing. Otherwise there was no point. So the fib of muses, long ago, had been cooked up, and the words to match. "Mousa-moisa-musa," he had groaned, as if hating the words themselves. "It all came down, it was handed down. You remember? Pieria, and the before-breakfast landing on Helicon, the mountain. The story that came out was that the muses had a *jour de fête* every four years at Thespiae. Just an undifferentiated bunch of goddesses having a high old time. You would not remember, I suppose. No, you would not. You weren't supposed to, signora. You were one of the original nine. Someone had said, apropos of a technological civilization such as ours, that minds ought to be able to go beyond mere reason. We never could, but we could perhaps entice some other beings into doing so. Well, we've been at it since long before Homer, and look how feebly *he* performed. One of your action poets, social history and bloody soldiery."

It was true. Every now and then she had had this fleeting intuition of having been somewhere else, doing something else such as teaching or making speeches. Once upon a time she had been a virgin, and then she had been made a virgin again during the unremembered, unthinkably long journey from Radius Edna, living entire lifetimes one after another in her coma, only to infiltrate poetry into the beings of an experimental planet. The question she had always put to herself was this: How, if none of us, the original nine, can remember what preceded our service here, how can we ever tell if the whole thing is a hoax? Am I an earthling muse, dreaming I was once an extraterrestrial, or am I truly an extraterrestrial only dreaming I am here, and responsible for so much verse? Am I only in someone else's dream, or is someone impersonating me in a dream of my own? It is all too far back, too dim. If I believe in all the statues, I believe in myself. I am having a life. We liked Milton for his love of astronomy—a touch of favoritism, no doubt. So what? It was strange: the race here managed to do all else under their own steam, but their poetry was otherworldly, grafted into them by such as herself, popularly known in the last phase of the journey here as two-handed engines: afflatus-spreaders, in other words, members of a celestial team destined to create poetry as a pet domesticated on a nearby planet, almost like a mistress in a love nest on the other side of town. Amazing how the locals took credit for their own poets, as if they had dreamed up the art for themselves. That it was all Radius-Ednaic they had no idea—and never would, unless an ecstatic decree came in at the speed of light, calling them to order. She had an acute sense of what she called ephemeral eternality, and wanted to die, as Milton would die, but her kind never did. Her old name had been Pomme.

Without the least vanity, she had always thought she was the perfect replica, concocted in mist, haze, and a silicon furnace so long ago, *before poetry.* Not only had she passed muster; she had seemed enough of an earthly goddess for there to have been rumors about her, all based on human misconduct. Only she, she thought, knew about the slight variations that could have got her into trouble. She had only one memory: of having seen a tree on Radius Edna bend away from her out of sheer courtesy. She tended to perspire from under her fingernails, as well as in the stock fashion. Under pressure, she could breathe through either ear, and had within her thorax the correct airways for this extraordinary feat. And she had a pylonidal cyst in the form of a human head, right at the top of the crease between her buttocks: a flaw in the manufacturing which, as she told herself, made her two, although even if there had been two hundred of her, she mourned, none of them would have known anything like personal fulfillment on the plane of love. Muses knew only the joy of achieving their mission—the two-handed engine in excelsis—and the temporary gratification of casual sex. Only with one another could they achieve any kind of ecstasy, but they rarely saw one another, being forever on extravagant urgent errands for their initiator teams back in the home galaxy. No one on earth had yet fathomed their true quality, these nine, if in doubt attributing their odd ways to their being Greek divinities, and to the dread power *Anangke* that in myth controlled even them.

On the littoral of an insentient nothing, she felt the ghost of an absence, one which, having been known, had moved as it were sideways, enabling other shades of meaning to thrive or, if not that, to assemble in meaning-less, dead echelon above a Thames seascape whose contours evoked the barrens and the fires in the margins of the universe where, doting on the word "be," she roamed on weekends, cosmically loafing, as unable to die as to change the absurdity of absence into the absurdity at the hardly beating heart of absence. Always, from her duties, she longed for fruition, to be in love. If the objects of her devotions fell in love with her, that was part of the preamble, but she herself remained passionately aloof, always on the verge. She saw herself as rapturously effusive, heartily caustic: an interesting mix of school-marm and holy ghost, bored suburban matron and fierce maenad. She was a dynamic modifier, sweeping the distance with an inbuilt glass but obliged to observe her quota of poets: only so many per century—an incredible restriction in someone whose metaphors struck humans as real. She had tried willing herself into infatuation, like a heart patient "bearing down" on the vagus nerve to make an atrial fibrillation quit, but nothing happened—nothing extreme, anyway. She had almost produced a quiver in herself when dealing with Catullus and Sappho, but she had long ago written off that sensation to bad temper (fury fanning lust on). She needed to cuddle, she told herself: simple stuff like hugs and strokes, but her body was immune and her mind was ponderously abstruse.

Only when another kind of two-handed engine, a swordsman, cut her in two, would she be able to take a little fondling, feel a little smitten. It would never happen, even though Milton exercised with a sword; he was too prudent, too demure, she thought. He would have to be instructed by Quiescan for, oh, several hundred years how to muster the strength to slice an ion torso in two.

One of these centuries, she knew, she would be withdrawn without warning, her tour of duty done, her time of childbearing on Radius Edna ready to begin. She knew no more than that. Some muses had vanished, evaporated, sucked back home for punishment or abolished here on Earth. She had no idea if she was getting straight A's or merely B's, but she suspected she was doing an average job, maybe no more than that. Volcanic in her midwifery, she treasured the faces of her poets, wondering if, at death, they were all mentally transported away from Earth to a profitable career in the Caustic Doldrums, where her home was. One day she would throw an enormous picnic for the entire team of experimental subjects, but only, she thought, when many generations of poets had petered out and some other mode, such as the novel, had taken over. Yet what could she expect of Earth, whose half-wits were subject to vulgarer fractions than the half-wits back home? Not allowed to compose verses herself, she felt chronically vicarious, at odds with the very doctrine she lived by. How she ached for dance, mime, or history, but there was no chopping and changing among muses; each had to honor her initial assignment and accept a nimbus in lieu of a pat on the back, sucking her spit to make a winsome noise.

So many things irked her, most of all her sense that, in the Radius Ednaic scheme of things, what she had been doing for centuries far from home amounted to very

little: a bagatelle from which, of course, she had learned
to love poetry and honor it, as the other muses had
learned to honor and love arts of their own. In Earthly
books she occupied a good deal of space; the beings there
had no idea what she was or whence she came, and
blithely swallowed propaganda about springs and pools.
Her impression was that no one really cared about the
truth. Earthlings just wanted a myth and that was that.
How fabulous the truth would have been to them, except
that it would have shattered their theologies. Back home,
she just knew it, she would earn a paragraph at most in
the Galactic Encyclopedia as one of nine, or a dozen, who
did a little experimental farming or seeding on a nearby
planet, to no great purpose or point except that the
subsequent growth, poetry, pleased just a few through
the centuries. *Miniatures:* she would be listed under that,
she thought. Or Minority Exports. Others had been
permitted to carve light or translate ideas into a new geol-
ogy, to disrupt neighboring suns or, at least, engage in
planet-forming on the grand scale. She and her cohorts
had managed something tiny, that was all, and therefore
merited something mighty in compensation. But life on
Radius Edna did not work like that, and the proposal to
install terrestrial poets in a special college there had
flopped. On death, she had suggested, they should be
photonically transported, but only a few wanted them, so
they were left to rot on Earth, like annuals; even the
apparent perennials, such as Shakespeare and Catullus,
were left where they fell. At least their souls were, like
their cadavers.

Irritated at such trifling with footling, and flooded with a certain honorable bigotry in behalf of poetry she rubbed one foot against the other, itching to be off, to ride the gondola toward poets of wit and brio. She had had enough, and of Milton, too; but she could not quite strip herself of the illusion that one day a poet she discovered, and maieutically made, would turn out to be the one who released her emotions in a torrent of tenderness. Should that happen on Earth, she would ask to stay, but she would be here for centuries yet, beginning each year to smell more and more of eucalyptus, not so much drying up as nimbly enlarging herself until, sometime in the twentieth century, she could be found in the stores devoted to large women. To be celestial yet so much of an everyday earthling piqued her. She wanted glamour; she adored the present tense (at which Catullus had been so good; *is* so good, she whispered); she longed for promotion, out of the realm of muses into something heroic: less the traveling saleslady, more the stroke of lightning that yielded the *liber fulguralis*, the lightning book. She prayed, she murmured the best lines of her protégés, she gazed skyward and offered herself to whatever force among the stars could use a woman of peripatetic talent and exquisite taste.

No use. With Quiescan, like a couple evicted from some seedy lodging for which they lacked the rent, she dawdled sulkily along the sand, stuck one foot over the side of the gondola, and gave up on the latest episode, already stamped in stone as it was, but finito, a problem to come for schoolboys, a hell for women.

As for young John Milton, she saw him in later years, a virtual skeleton in a rocking chair, fondling a length of material—chinoiserie—twice as long as he was tall: evaluating a winding sheet that embodied all the gorgeousness he had eyed, his expression one of forlorn ecstasy. It was clear that he had seen Trodochian fireships exploding in the region of the Hyades, the rainbow shawls of young Radius Edna maidens being unfurled from them before sacrifice, the chromatic stipple of college scarves worn by the most brilliant young students, known as Pdonts (red and yellow, blue and white the most famous combinations for the two best colleges at the planetary university—Envenobia and Dolst).

Milton was looking with affection at his own death, still yearning to be of tender service to his long-gone

Amaryllis: to massage her feet, to kiss her eyelids closed, to smooth out with a flat hand the black velvet of her stomach. Where had she gone, what had she become? By then he had learned the faces of the other muses by heart: the plump and slightly equine one with lips so out-pulped and tender they would bleed at the merest touch; the Aryan-nosed one forever trying on a crown with a look of downcast impenitence; the bony-jawed, peering one whose mouth remained always shut; the one who crouched full of misgiving, her lips puckered in for something lost, ruined, longed-for. All white except for the irradiated, charcoal one exiled to a Black Sea of her own because too awful to look at, but by earthly standards a beauty, to Milton above all, who loved her because she was left-handed, smelled of eucalyptus, and had a voice—oh, that voice—of a sleepy spaceship commander growing bored out among the Pleiades, with haughty tedium settling into her voice, a matron balm tinctured with faintest petulance, a hint of snarl. Had the voice fallen through holes gnawed in the chinoiserie? Rats? Sunspots? Moths? Dunefondlers or swonts? By whose creatures where?

She had to go, Zeus love him. These visual premonitions meant she would never see him again, the pet of the moment, and this pained her like teething. I am delicate, brazen, she told herself; I have eternal repute. Off, then, and bastards be cherished.

As THEY WENT, MILTON CAPERED UP AND DOWN THE narrow beach howling, seizing handfuls of wet sand and plastering his face, getting it in his eyes the worse to see. He called out over the sea, then toward land, beating his fists against his chest, unable to believe that a one-day bond could feel so lately gorgeous. To be so previous had not been allowed, therefore to be so dashed by its vanishing was daft. All his wise words to himself he threw away. The gondola had already gone into the acrid mist. No moon shone, no light beckoned.

After running up and down, he took to pacing, and then stood still, waiting to be struck by lightning, turned to salt, felled by a monster of sleep. Nothing began. London was not his, though he knew the way to it. Poetry was not his, any more than the image of her was his alone. Calling her name, he made himself hoarse, volunteering to be her next Quiescan, even to be mutilated. Nothing came thundering toward him, though, and, knowing he was a broken youth, he faced the water, then turned left inland, braving marsh and nightgas in order to return to Cambridge on March the nineteenth, where his new tutor, Nathaniel Tovey, awaited him.